Henry James OM (15 April 1843 – 28 February 1916) was an American-British author regarded as a key transitional figure between literary realism and literary modernism, and is considered by many to be among the greatest novelists in the English language. He was the son of Henry James Sr. and the brother of renowned philosopher and psychologist William James and diarist Alice James.

He is best known for a number of novels dealing with the social and marital interplay between émigré Americans, English people, and continental Europeans. Examples of such novels include The Portrait of a Lady, The Ambassadors, and The Wings of the Dove. His later works were increasingly experimental. In describing the internal states of mind and social dynamics of his characters, James often made use of a style in which ambiguous or contradictory motives and impressions were overlaid or juxtaposed in the discussion of a character's psyche.(Source: Wikipedia)

Literary works:
Watch and Ward (1871)
Roderick Hudson (1875)
The American (1877)
The Europeans (1878)
Confidence (1879)
Washington Square (1880)
The Portrait of a Lady (1881)
The Bostonians (1886)
The Princess Casamassima (1886)
The Reverberator (1888)
The Tragic Muse (1890)
The Other House (1896)
The Spoils of Poynton (1897)
What Maisie Knew (1897)

WITHIN THE RIM

HENRY JAMES

PRINCE CLASSICS

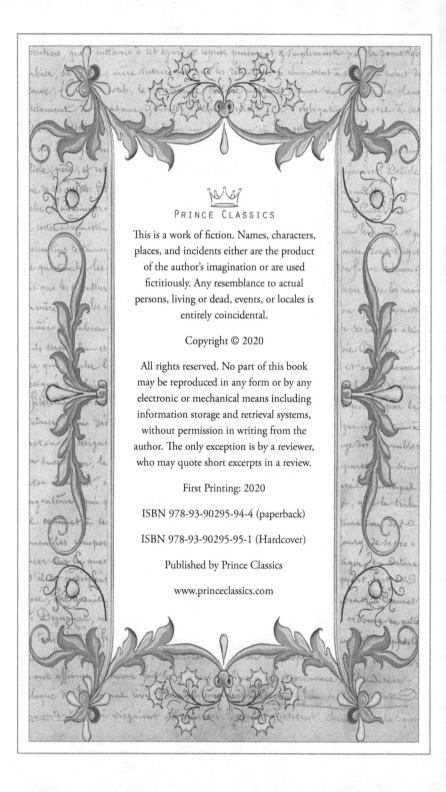

First Printing: 2020

ISBN 978-93-90295-94-4 (paperback)

ISBN 978-93-90295-95-1 (Hardcover)

Published by Prince Classics

www.princeclassics.com

Contents

WITHIN THE RIM

WITHIN THE RIM

THE first sense of it all to me after the first shock and horror was that of a sudden leap back into life of the violence with which the American Civil War broke upon us, at the North, fifty-four years ago, when I had a consciousness of youth which perhaps equalled in vivacity my present consciousness of age. The illusion was complete, in its immediate rush; everything quite exactly matched in the two cases; the tension of the hours after the flag of the Union had been fired upon in South Carolina living again, with a tragic strangeness of recurrence, in the interval during which the fate of Belgium hung in the scales and the possibilities of that of France looked this country harder in the face, one recognised, than any possibility, even that of the England of the Armada, even that of the long Napoleonic menace, could be imagined to have looked her. The analogy quickened and deepened with every elapsing hour; the drop of the balance under the invasion of Belgium reproduced with intensity the agitation of the New England air by Mr Lincoln's call to arms, and I went about for a short space as with the queer secret locked in my breast of at least already knowing how such occasions helped and what a big war was going to mean. That this was literally a light in the darkness, or that it materially helped the prospect to be considered, is perhaps more than I can say; but it at least added the strangest of savours, an inexpressible romantic thrill, to the harsh taste of the crisis: I found myself literally knowing 'by experience' what immensities, what monstrosities, what revelations of what immeasurabilities, our affair would carry in its bosom—a knowledge that flattered me by its hint of immunity from illusion. The sudden new tang in the atmosphere, the flagrant difference, as one noted, in the look of everything, especially in that of people's faces, the expressions, the hushes, the clustered groups, the detached wanderers and slow-paced public meditators, were so many impressions long before received and in which the stretch of more than half a century had still left a sharpness. So I took the case in and drew a vague comfort, I can scarce say why, from recognition; so, while recognition lasted, I found it come home to me that we, we of the ancient day, had known, had tremendously learnt, what the awful business is when it is 'long,' when it remains for months and months bitter and arid, void even of any great honour. In consequence of which, under the rapid rise of presumptions of difficulty, to whatever effect of dismay or of excitement, my possession of something like a standard of difficulty, and, as I might perhaps feel too, of success, became in its way a private luxury.

My point is, however, that upon this luxury I was allowed after all but ever so scantily to feed. I am unable to say when exactly it was that the rich analogy, the fine and sharp identity between the faded and the vivid case broke down, with the support obscurely derived from them; the moment anyhow came soon enough at which experience felt the ground give way and that one swung off into space, into history, into darkness, with every lamp extinguished and every abyss gaping. It ceased quite to matter for reassurance that the victory of the North had been so delayed and yet so complete, that our struggle had worn upon the world of the time, and quite to exasperation, as could well be remembered, by its length; if the present complication should but begin to be as long as it was broad no term of comparison borrowed from the past would so much as begin to fit it. I might have found it humiliating; in fact, however, I found it of the most commanding interest, whether at certain hours of dire apprehension or at certain others of the finer probability, that the biggest like convulsion our generations had known was still but too clearly to be left far behind for exaltations and terrors, for effort and result, as a general exhibition of the perversity of nations and of the energy of man. Such at least was the turn the comparison took at a given moment in a remembering mind that had been steeped, so far as its restricted contact went, but in the Northern story; I did, I confess, cling awhile to the fancy that what loomed perhaps for England, what already did so much more than loom for crucified Belgium, what was let loose in a torrent upon indestructible France, might correspond more or less with the pressure of the old terrible time as the fighting South had had to know it, and with the grim conditions under which she had at last given way. For the rest of the matter, as I say, the difference of aspect produced by the difference of intensity cut short very soon my vision of similitude. The intensity swallowed up everything; the rate and the scale and the speed, the unprecedented engines, the vast incalculable connections, the immediate presence, as it were, of France and Belgium, whom one could hear pant, through the summer air, in their effort and their alarm, these things, with the prodigious might of the enemy added, made me say, dropping into humility in a manner that resembled not a little a drop into still greater depths, 'Oh, no, that surely can't have been "a patch" on this!' Which conclusion made accordingly for a new experience altogether, such as I gratefully embrace here an occasion not to leave unrecorded.

It was in the first place, after the strangest fashion, a sense of the extraordinary way in which the most benign conditions of light and air, of sky and sea, the most beautiful English summer conceivable, mixed themselves with all the violence of action and passion, the other so hideous and piteous, so heroic and tragic facts, and flouted them as with the example of something far superior. Never were desperate doings so blandly lighted up as by the two unforgettable months that I was to spend so much of in looking over from the old rampart of a little high-perched Sussex town at the bright blue streak of the Channel, within a mile or two of us at its nearest point, the point to which it had receded after washing our rock-base in its earlier ages, and staring at the bright mystery beyond the rim of the farthest opaline reach. Just on the other side of that finest of horizon-lines history was raging at a pitch new under the sun; thinly masked by that shameless smile the Belgian horror grew; the curve of the globe toward these things was of the scantest, and yet the hither spaces of the purest, the interval representing only charm and calm and ease. One grew to feel that the nearer elements, those of land and water and sky at their loveliest, were making thus, day after day, a particular prodigious point, insisting in their manner on a sense and a wondrous story which it would be the restless watcher's fault if he didn't take in. Not that these were hints or arts against which he was in the least degree proof; they penetrated with every hour deeper into the soul, and, the contemplations I speak of aiding, irresistibly worked out an endless volume of references. It was all somehow the history of the hour addressing itself to the individual mind—or to that in any case of the person, at once so appalled and so beguiled, of whose response to the whole appeal I attempt this brief account. Round about him stretched the scene of his fondest frequentation as time had determined the habit; but it was as if every reason and every sentiment conducing to the connection had, under the shock of events, entered into solution with every other, so that the only thinkable approach to rest, that is to the recovery of an inward order, would be in restoring them each, or to as many as would serve the purpose, some individual dignity and some form.

It came indeed largely of itself, my main help to the reparatory, the re-identifying process; came by this very chance that in the splendour of the season there was no mistaking the case or the plea. 'This, as you can see better than ever before,' the elements kept conspiring to say, 'is the rare, the sole, the exquisite England whose weight now hangs in the balance, and your appreciation of whose value, much as in the easy years you may have taken it for granted, seems exposed to some fresh and strange and strong determinant, something that breaks in like a character of high colour in a play.' Nothing could have thrilled me more, I recognise, than the threat of this irruption or than the dramatic pitch; yet a degree of pain attached to the ploughed-up state it implied—so that, with an elderly dread of a waste of emotion, I fear I almost pusillanimously asked myself why a sentiment from so far back recorded as lively should need to become any livelier, and in fact should hesitate to beg off from the higher diapason. I felt as the quiet dweller in a tenement so often feels when the question of 'structural improvements' is thrust upon him; my house of the spirit, amid everything about me, had become more and more the inhabited, adjusted, familiar home, quite big enough and sound enough for the spirit's uses and with any intrinsic inconvenience corrected only since by that principle's having cultivated and formed, at whatever personal cost (since my spirit was essentially a person), the right habits, and so settled into the right attitude for practical, for contented occupation. If, however, such was my vulgar apprehension, as I put it, the case was taken out of my hands by the fate that so often deals with these accidents, and I found myself before long building on additions and upper storys, throwing out extensions and protrusions, indulging even, all recklessly, in gables and pinnacles and battlements—things that had presently transformed the unpretending place into I scarce know what to call it, a fortress of the faith, a palace of the soul, an extravagant, bristling, flag-flying structure which had quite as much to do with the air as with the earth. And all this, when one came to return upon it in a considering or curious way, because to and fro one kept going on the old rampart, the town 'look-out,' to spend one's aching wonder again and again on the bright sky-line that at once held and mocked it. Just over that line were unutterable things, massacre and ravage and anguish, all but irresistible assault and cruelty, bewilderment and heroism all but overwhelmed; from the sense of which one had but to turn one's head to take in something unspeakably different and that yet produced, as by some extraordinary paradox, a pang almost as sharp.

It was of course by the imagination that this latter was quickened to an intensity thus akin to pain—but the imagination had doubtless at every turn, without exception, more to say to one's state of mind, and dealt more with the whole unfolding scene, than any other contributive force. Never in all my life, probably, had I been so glad to have opened betimes an account with this faculty and to be able to feel for the most part something to my credit there; so vivid I mean had to be one's prevision of the rate at which drafts on that source would require cashing. All of which is a manner of saying that in face of what during those horrible days seemed exactly over the way the old inviolate England, as to whom the fact that she *was* inviolate, in every valid sense of the term, had become, with long acquaintance, so common and dull, suddenly shone in a light never caught before and which was for the next weeks, all the magnificence of August and September, to reduce a thousand things to a sort of merciless distinctness. It was not so much that they leaped forth, these things, under the particular recognition, as that they multiplied without end and abounded, always in some association at least that caught the eye, all together overscoring the image as a whole or causing the old accepted synthesis to bristle with accents. The image as a whole, thus richly made up of them—or of the numberless testifying touches to the effect that we were not there on our sea defence as the other, the harried, countries were behind such bulwarks as they could throw up—was the central fact of consciousness and the one to which every impression and every apprehension more or less promptly related themselves; it made of itself the company in which for the time the mind most naturally and yet most importunately lived. One walked of course in the shade of the ambiguous contrast—ambiguous because of the dark question of whether it was the liabilities of Belgium and France, to say nothing of their awful actualities, that made England's state so rare, or

England's state that showed her tragic sisters for doubly outraged; the action of the matter was at least that of one's feeling in one's hand and weighing it there with the last tenderness, for fullest value, the golden key that unlocked every compartment of the English character.

Clearly this general mystery or mixture was to be laid open under stress of fortune as never yet—the unprecedentedness was above all what came over us again and again, armaments unknown to human experience looming all the while larger and larger; but whatever face or succession of faces the genius of the race should most turn up the main mark of them all would be in the difference that, taken together, couldn't fail to keep them more unlike the peoples off there beyond than any pair even of the most approved of these peoples are unlike each other. 'Insularity!'—one had spent no small part of one's past time in mocking or in otherwise fingering the sense out of that word; yet here it was in the air wherever one looked and as stuffed with meaning as if nothing had ever worn away from it, as if its full force on the contrary amounted to inward congestion. What the term essentially signified was in the oddest way a question at once enormous and irrelevant; what it might *show* as signifying, what it was in the circumstances actively and most probably going to, seemed rather the true consideration, indicated with all the weight of the evidence scattered about. Just the fixed *look* of England under the August sky, what was this but the most vivid exhibition of character conceivable and the face turned up, to repeat my expression, with a frankness that really left no further inquiry to be made? That appearance was of the exempt state, the record of the long safe centuries, in its happiest form, and even if any shade of happiness at such an hour might well seem a sign of profanity or perversity. To *that* there were all sorts of things to say, I could at once reflect, however; wouldn't it be the thing supremely in character that England should look most complacently herself, irradiating all her reasons for it, at the very crisis of the question of the true toughness, in other words the further duration, of her identity? I might observe, as for that matter I repeatedly and unspeakably did while the two months lasted, that she was pouring forth this identity, as atmosphere and aspect and picture, in the very measure and to the very top of her consciousness of how it hung in the balance. Thus one arrived, through the succession of shining days, at the finest sense of the case—the interesting truth that her consciously not being as her tragic sisters were in the great particular was virtually just her genius, and that the very straightest thing she could do would naturally be not to flinch at the dark hour from any profession of her genius. Looking myself more askance at the dark hour (politically speaking I mean) than I after my fashion figured her as doing in her mass, I found it of an extreme, of quite an endless fascination to trace as many as possible of her felt idiosyncrasies back to her settled sea-confidence, and to see this now in turn account for so many other things, the smallest as well as the biggest, that, to give the fewest hints of illustration, the mere spread of the great trees, the mere gathers in the little bluey-white curtains of the cottage windows, the mere curl of the tinted smoke from the old chimneys matching that note, became a sort of exquisite evidence.

Exquisite evidence of a like general class, it was true, didn't on the other side of the Channel prevent the awful liability to the reach of attack—its having borne fruit and been corrected or averted again was in fact what half the foreign picture meant; but the foreign genius was the other, other at almost every point; it had always in the past and on the spot, one remembered, expressed things, confessed things, with a difference, and part of that difference was of course the difference of history: the fact of exemption, as I have called it, the fact that a blest inviolacy was almost exactly what had least flourished. France and Belgium, to refer only to them, became dear accordingly, in the light I speak of, because, having suffered and suffered, they were suffering yet again, while precisely the opposite process worked for the scene directly beneath my eyes. England was interesting, to put it mildly—which is but a shy evasion of putting it passionately—because she hadn't suffered, because there were passages of that sort she had publicly declined and defied; at the same time that one wouldn't have the case so simple as to set it down wholly to her luck. France and Belgium, for the past, confessed, to repeat my term; while England, so consistently harmonised, with all her long unbrokenness thick and rich upon her, seemed never to do that, nor to need it, in order to practise on a certain fine critical, not to mention a certain fine prejudiced, sensibility. It was the season of sensibility now, at any rate for just those days and just that poor place of yearning, of merely yearning, vigil;

15

and I may add with all emphasis that never had I had occasion so to learn how far sensibility may go when once well wound up. It was saying little to say I did justice easiest at once and promptest to the most advertised proposal of the enemy, his rank intention of clapping down the spiked helmet, than which no form of headgear, by the way, had ever struck one as of a more graceless, a more tell-tale platitude, upon the priceless genius of France; far from new, after all, was that measure of the final death in him of the saving sense of proportion which only gross dementia can abolish. Those of my generation who could remember the detected and frustrated purpose of a renewed Germanic pounce upon the country which, all but bled to death in 1871, had become capable within five years of the most penetrating irony of revival ever recorded, were well aware of how in that at once sinister and grotesque connection they had felt notified in time. It was the extension of the programme and its still more prodigious publication during the quarter of a century of interval, it was the announced application of the extinguisher to the quite other, the really so contrasted genius the expression of which surrounded me in the manner I have glanced at, it was the extraordinary fact of a declared non-sufferance any longer, on Germany's part, of either of the obnoxious national forms disfiguring her westward horizon, and even though by her own allowance they had nothing intellectually or socially in common save that they were objectionable and, as an incident, crushable—it was this, I say, that gave one furiously to think, or rather, while one thanked one's stars for the luxury, furiously and all but unutterably to feel.

The beauty and the interest, the now more than ever copious and welcome expression, of the aspects nearest me found their value in their being so resistingly, just to that very degree of eccentricity, with that very density of home-grownness, what they were; in the same way as the character of the sister-land lately joined in sisterhood showed for exquisite because so ingrained and incorrigible, so beautifully all her own and inimitable on other ground. If it would have been hard really to give the measure of one's dismay at the awful proposition of a world squeezed together in the huge Prussian fist and with the variety and spontaneity of its parts oozing in a steady trickle, like the sacred blood of sacrifice, between those hideous knuckly fingers, so, none the less, every reason with which our preference for a better condition and a nobler fate could possibly bristle kept battering at my heart, kept, in fact, pushing into it, after the fashion of a crowd of the alarmed faithful at the door of a church. The effect was literally, yes, as of the occasion of some great religious service, with prostrations and exaltations, the light of a thousand candles and the sound of soaring choirs—all of which figured one's individual inward state as determined by the menace. One could still note at the same time, however, that this high pitch of private emotion was by itself far from meeting the case as the enemy presented it; what I wanted, of course, to do was to meet it with the last lucidity, the fullest support for particular defensive pleas or claims—and this even if what most underlay all such without exception came back to my actual vision, that and no more, of the general sense of the land. The vision was fed, and fed to such a tune that in the quest for reasons—that is, for the particulars of one's affection, the more detailed the better—the blades of grass, the outlines of leaves, the drift of clouds, the streaks of mortar between old bricks, not to speak of the call of child-voices muffled in the comforting air, became, as I have noted, with a hundred other like touches, casually felt, extraordinary admonitions and symbols, close links of a tangible chain. When once the question fairly hung there of the possibility, more showily set forth than it had up to then presumed to be, of a world without use for the tradition so embodied, an order substituting for this, by an unmannerly thrust, quite another and really, it would seem, quite a ridiculous, a crudely and clumsily improvised story, we might all have resembled together a group of children at their nurse's knee disconcerted by some tale that it isn't their habit to hear. We loved the old tale, or at least I did, exactly because I knew it; which leaves me keen to make the point, none the less, that my appreciation of the case for world-variety found the deeply and blessedly familiar perfectly consistent with it. This came of what I 'read into' the familiar; and of what I did so read, of what I kept reading through that uplifted time, these remarks were to have attempted a record that has reached its limit sooner than I had hoped.

I was not then to the manner born, but my apprehension of what it was on the part of others to be so had been confirmed and enriched by the long years, and I gave myself up to the general, the native image I thus circled around as to the dearest and most precious of all native images. That verily became at the crisis an occupation sublime; which was not, after all, so much an earnest study or fond arrangement of the mixed aspects as a positive, a fairly sensual bask in their light, too kindled and too rich not to pour out by its own force. The strength and the copious play of the appearances acting in this collective fashion carried everything before them; no dark discrimination, no stiff little reserve that one might ever have made, stood up in the diffused day for a moment. It was in the opposite way, the most opposite possible, that one's intelligence worked, all along the line; so that with the warmth of the mere sensation that 'they' were about as good, above all when it came to the stress, as could well be expected of people, there was the acute interest of the successive points at which one recognised why. This last, the satisfaction of the deepened intelligence, turned, I may frankly say, to a prolonged revel—'they' being the people about me and every comfort I had ever had of them smiling its individual smile straight at me and conducing to an effect of candour that is beyond any close notation. They didn't know how good they were, and their candour had a peculiar lovability of unconsciousness; one had more imagination at their service in this cause than they had in almost any cause of their own; it was wonderful, it was beautiful, it was inscrutable, that they could make one feel this and yet not feel with it that it at all practically diminished them. Of course, if a shade should come on occasion to fall across the picture, that shade would perhaps be the question whether the most restless of the faculties mightn't on the whole too much fail them. It beautified life, I duly remembered, it promoted art, it inspired faith, it crowned conversation, but hadn't it—always again under stress—still finer applications than these, and mightn't it in a word, taking the right direction, peculiarly conduce to virtue? Wouldn't it, indeed, be indispensable to virtue of the highest strain? Never mind, at any rate—so my emotion replied; with it or without it we seemed to *be* taking the right direction; moreover, the next best thing to the imagination people may have, if they can, is the quantity of it they may set going in others, and which, imperfectly aware, they are just exposed to from such others, and must make the best of: their advantage becoming simply that it works, for the connection, all in their favour. That of the associated outsider, the order of whose feelings, for the occasion, I have doubtless not given a wholly lucid sketch of, cultivated its opportunity week after week at such a rate that, technical alien as he was, the privilege of the great partaking, of shared instincts and ideals, of a communion of race and tongue, temper and tradition, put on before all the blest appearances a splendour to which I hoped that so long as I might yet live my eyes would never grow dim. And the great intensity, the melting together of the spiritual sources so loosed in a really intoxicating draught, was when I shifted my watch from near east to far west and caught the enemy, who seemed ubiquitous, in the long-observed effort that most fastened on him the insolence of his dream and the depth of his delusion. There in the west were those of my own fond fellowship, the other, the ready and rallying partakers, and it was on the treasure of our whole unquenchable association that in the riot of his ignorance—this at least apparently armour-proof—he had laid his unholy hands.

REFUGEES IN CHELSEA

THIS is not a Report on our so interesting and inspiring Chelsea work, since November last, in aid of the Belgians driven thither from their country by a violence of unprovoked invasion and ravage more appalling than has ever before overtaken a peaceful and industrious people; it is the simple statement of a neighbour and an observer deeply affected by the most tragic exhibition of national and civil prosperity and felicity suddenly subjected to bewildering outrage that it would have been possible to conceive. The case, as the generous American communities have shown they well understand, has had no analogue in the experience of our modern generations, no matter how far back we go; it has been recognised, in surpassing practical ways, as virtually the greatest public horror of our age, or of all the preceding; and one gratefully feels, in presence of so much done in direct mitigation of it, that its appeal to the pity and the indignation of the civilised world anticipated and transcended from the first all superfluity of argument. We live into—that is, we learn to cultivate—possibilities of sympathy and reaches of beneficence very much as the stricken and suffering themselves live into their dreadful history and explore and reveal its extent; and this admirable truth it is that unceasingly pleads with the intelligent, the fortunate, and the exempt, not to consent in advance to any dull limitation of the helpful idea. The American people have surely a genius, of the most eminent kind, for withholding any such consent and despising all such limits; and there is doubtless no remarked connection in which they have so shown the sympathetic imagination in free and fearless activity—that is, in high originality—as under the suggestion of the tragedy of Belgium.

I have small warrant perhaps to say that atmospheres are communicable; but I can testify at least that they are breathable on the spot, to whatever effect of depression or of cheer; and I should go far, I feel, were I to attempt to register the full bitter-sweet taste, by our Chelsea waterside, all these months, of the refugee element in our vital medium. (The sweet, as I strain a point perhaps to call it, inheres, to whatever distinguishability, in our hope of having really done something, verily done much; the bitter ineradicably seasons the consciousness, hopes and demonstrations and fond presumptions and all.) I need go no further, none the less, than the makeshift provisional gates of Crosby Hall, marvellous monument transplanted a few years since from the Bishopsgate quarter of the City to a part of the ancient suburban site of the garden of Sir Thomas More, and now serving with extraordinary beneficence as the most splendid of shelters for the homeless. This great private structure, though of the grandest civic character, dating from the fifteenth century, and one of the noblest relics of the past that London could show, was held a few years back so to cumber the precious acre or more on which it stood that it was taken to pieces in the candid commercial interest and in order that the site it had so long sanctified should be converted to such uses as would stuff out still further the ideal number of private pockets. Dismay and disgust were unable to save it; the most that could be done was to gather in with tenderness of care its innumerable constituent parts and convey them into safer conditions, where a sad defeated piety has been able to re-edify them into some semblance of the original majesty. Strange withal some of the turns of the whirligig of time; the priceless structure came down to the sound of lamentation, not to say of execration, and of the gnashing of teeth, and went up again before cold and disbelieving, quite despairing, eyes; in spite of which history appears to have decided once more to cherish it and give a new consecration. It is, in truth, still magnificent; it lives again for our gratitude in its noblest particulars; and the almost incomparable roof has arched all this winter and spring over a scene probably more interesting and certainly more pathetic than any that have ever drawn down its ancient far-off blessing.

The place has formed, then, the headquarters of the Chelsea circle of hospitality to the exiled, the broken, and the bewildered; and if I may speak of having taken home the lesson of their state and the sense of their story, it is by meeting them in the finest club conditions conceivable that I have been able to do so. Hither, month after month and day after day, the unfortunates have flocked, each afternoon; and here the comparatively exempt, almost ashamed of their exemption in presence of so much woe, have made them welcome to every form of succour and reassurance. Certain afternoons each week have worn the character of the huge comprehensive tea-party, a fresh well-wisher discharging the social and financial cost of the fresh occasion—which has always festally profited, in addition, by the extraordinary command of musical accomplishment, the high standard of execution, that is the mark of the Belgian people. This exhibition of our splendid local resource has rested, of course, on a multitude of other resources, still local, but of a more intimate hospitality, little by little worked out and applied, and into the details of which I may not here pretend to go beyond noting that they have been accountable for the large housed and fed and clothed and generally protected and administered numbers, all provided for in Chelsea and its outer fringe, on which our scheme of sociability at Crosby Hall itself has up to now been able to draw. To have seen this scheme so long in operation has been to find it suggest many reflections, all of the most poignant and moving order; the foremost of which has, perhaps, had for its subject that never before can the wanton hand of history have descended upon a group of communities less expectant of public violence from without or less prepared for it and attuned to it.

The bewildered and amazed passivity of the Flemish civil population, the state as of people surprised by sudden ruffians, murderers, and thieves in the dead of night and hurled out, terrified and half clad, snatching at the few scant household gods nearest at hand, into a darkness mitigated but by flaring incendiary torches—this has been the experience stamped on our scores and scores of thousands, whose testimony to suffering, dismay, and despoilment silence alone, the silence of vain uncontributive wonderment, has for the most part been able to express. Never was such a revelation of a deeply domestic, a rootedly domiciled and instinctively and separately clustered people, a mass of communities for which the sight of the home violated, the objects helping to form it profaned, and the cohesive family, the Belgian ideal of the constituted life, dismembered, disembowelled, and shattered, had so supremely to represent the crack of doom and the end of everything. There have been days and days when under this particular impression the mere aspect and manner of our serried recipients of relief, something vague and inarticulate as in persons who have given up everything but patience and are living, from hour to hour, but in the immediate and the unexplained, has put on such a pathos as to make the heart sick. One has had just to translate any seated row of figures, thankful for warmth and light and covering, for sustenance and human words and human looks, into terms that would exemplify some like exiled and huddled and charity-fed predicament for our superior selves, to feel our exposure to such a fate, our submission to it, our holding in the least together under it, darkly unthinkable. Dim imaginations would at such moments interpose, a confused theory that even at the worst our adventurous habits, our imperial traditions, our general defiance of the superstition of domesticity, would dash from our lips the cup of bitterness; from these it was at all events impossible not to come back to the consciousness that almost every creature there collected was indebted to our good offices for the means to come at all. I thought of our parents and children, our brothers and sisters, aligned in borrowed garments and settled to an as yet undetermined future of eleemosynary tea and buns, and I ask myself, doubtless to little purpose, either what grace of resignation or what clamour of protest we should, beneath the same star, be noted as substituting for the inveterate Belgian decency.

I can only profess at once that the sense of this last round about one was, at certain hours when the music and the chant of consolation rose in the stillness from our improvised stage at the end of the great hall, a thing to cloud with tears any pair of eyes lifted to our sublime saved roof in thanks for its vast comprehension. Questions of exhibited type, questions as to a range of form and tradition, a measure of sensibility and activity, not our own, dwindled and died before the gross fact of our having here an example of such a world-tragedy as we supposed Europe had outlived, and that nothing at all therefore mattered but that we should bravely and handsomely hold up our quite heavy enough end of it. It is because we have responded in this degree to the call unprecedented that we are, in common with a vast number of organisations scattered through these islands, qualified to claim that no small part of the inspiration to our enormous act of welcome resides in the moral interest it yields. One can indeed be certain of such a source of profit but in the degree in which one has found oneself personally drawing upon it; yet it is obvious that we are not treated every day to the disclosure of a national character, a national temperament and type, confined for the time to their plainest and stoutest features and set, on a prodigious scale, in all the relief that the strongest alien air and alien conditions can give them. Great salience, in such a case, do all collective idiosyncrasies acquire—upon the fullest enumeration of which, however, as the Belgian instance and the British atmosphere combine to represent them, I may not now embark, prepossessed wholly as I am with the more generally significant social stamp and human aspect so revealed, and with the quality derived from these things by the multiplied examples that help us to take them in. This feeling that our visitors illustrate above all the close and comfortable household life, with every implication of a seated and saturated practice of it, practice of the intimate and private and personal, the securely sensual and genial arts that flow from it, has been by itself the key to a plenitude of observation and in particular to as much friendly searching insight as one could desire to enjoy.

The moving, the lacerating thing is the fashion after which such a reading of the native elements, once adopted, has been as a light flaring into every obscurest retreat, as well as upon any puzzling ambiguity, of the state of shock of the national character under the infamy of the outrage put upon it. That *they*, of all people the most given over to local and patriarchal beatitude among the admirable and the cherished objects handed down to them by their so interesting history on every spot where its action has been thickest— that is, on every inch, so to speak, of their teeming territory—should find themselves identified with the most shamelessly cynical public act of which the civilised world at this hour retains the memory, is a fact truly representing the exquisite in the horrible; so peculiarly addressed has been their fate to the desecration of ideals that had fairly become breath of their lungs and flesh of their flesh. Oh, the installed and ensconced, the immemorially edified and arranged, the thoroughly furnished and provided and nourished people!— not in the least besotted or relaxed in their security and density, like the self-smothered society of the ancient world upon which the earlier Huns and Vandals poured down, but candidly complacent and admirably intelligent in their care for their living tradition, and only so off their guard as to have consciously set the example of this care to all such as had once smoked with them their wondrous pipe of peace. Almost any posture of stupefaction would have been conceivable in the shaken victims of this delusion: I can speak best, however, but of what I have already glanced at, that temperamental weight

24

of their fall which has again and again, at sight of many of them gathered together, made the considering heart as heavy for them as if it, too, had for the time been worsted.

However, it would take me far to tell of half the penetrating admonitions, whether of the dazed or of the roused appearance, that have for so long almost in like degree made our attention ache. I think of particular faces, in the whole connection, when I want most to remember—since to remember always, and never, never to forget, is a prescription shining before us like a possible light of dawn—faces saying such things in their silence, or in their speech of quite different matters, as to make the only thinkable comment or response some word or some gesture of reprieve to dumb or to dissimulated anguish. Blest be the power that has given to civilised men the appreciation of the face—such an immeasurable sphere of exercise for it has this monstrous trial of the peoples come to supply. Such histories, such a record of moral experience, of emotion convulsively suppressed, as one meets in some of them: and this even if, on the whole, one has been able to think of these special allies, all sustainingly, much rather as the sturdiest than as the most demonstrative of sufferers. I have in these rapid remarks to reduce my many impressions to the fewest, but must even thus spare one of them for commemoration of the admirable cast of working countenance we are rewarded by the sight of, wherever we turn amid the quantity of helpful service and all the fruitful industries that we have been able to start and that keep themselves going. These are the lights in the picture; and who indeed would wish that the lights themselves should be anything less than tragic? The strong young man (no young men are familiarly stronger,) mutilated, amputated, dismembered in penalty for their defence of their soil against the horde, and now engaged at Crosby Hall in the making of handloom socks, to whom I pay an occasional visit—much more for my own cheer, I apprehend, than for theirs—express so in their honest concentration under difficulties the actual and general value of their people that just to be in their presence is a blest renewal of faith. Excellent, exemplary, is this manly, homely, handy type, grave in its somewhat strained attention, but at once lighted to the briefest, sincerest humour of protest by any direct reference to the general cruelty of its misfortune. Anything but unsuggestive, the range of the 'quiet' physiognomy, when one feels the

25

consciousness behind it not to have run thin. Thick and strong is the good Flemish sense of life and all its functions—which fact is responsible for no empty and really unmodelled 'mug.'

I am afraid at the same time that, if the various ways of being bad are beyond our reckoning, the condition and the action of exemplary goodness tend rather to reduce to a certain rich unity of appearance those marked by them, however dissociated from each other such persons may have been by race and education. Otherwise what tribute shouldn't I be moved to pay to the gentleman of Flanders to whom the specially improvised craftsmen I have just mentioned owe their training and their inspiration? through *his* having, in his proscribed and denuded state, mastered the craft in order to recruit them to it, and, in fine, so far as my observation has been concerned, exhibit clear human virtue, courage and patience and the humility of sought fellowship in privation, with an unconscious beauty that I should be ashamed in this connection not to have noted publicly. I scarce know what such a 'personality' as his suggests to me if not that we had all, on our good Chelsea ground, best take up and cherish as directly and ultimately as possible every scrap of our community with our gentleman of Flanders. I make such a point as this, at the same time, only to remember how, almost wherever I have tried sustainingly to turn, my imagination and my intelligence have been quickened, and to recognise in particular, for that matter, that this couldn't possibly be more the case for them than in visiting a certain hostel in one of our comparatively contracted but amply decent local squares—riverside Chelsea having, of course, its own urban identity in the multitudinous County of London: which, in itself as happy an example, doubtless, of the hostel smoothly working as one need cite, placed me in grateful relation with a lady, one of the victims of her country's convulsion and in charge of the establishment I allude to, whom simply to 'meet,' as we say, is to learn how singular a dignity, how clear a distinction, may shine in active fortitude and economic self-effacement under an all but crushing catastrophe. 'Talk about faces——!' I could but privately ejaculate as I gathered the sense of all that this one represented in the way of natural nobleness and sweetness, a whole past acquaintance with letters and art and taste, insisting on their present restrictedness to bare sisterly service.

The proud rigour of association with pressing service alone, with absolutely nothing else, the bare commodious house, so otherwise known to me of old and now—like most of our hostels, if I am not mistaken, the most unconditioned of loans from its relinquishing owner—the lingering look of ancient peace in the precincts, an element I had already, as I passed and repassed at the afternoon hour, found somehow not at all dispelled by the presence in the central green garden itself of sundry maimed and hobbling and smiling convalescents from an extemporised small hospital close at hand, their battered khaki replaced by a like uniformity of the loose light blue, and friendly talk with them through the rails of their enclosure as blest to one participant at least as friendly talk with them always and everywhere is: such were the hovering elements of an impression in which the mind had yet mainly to yield to that haunting force on the part of our waiting proscripts which never consents to be long denied. The proof of which universally recognised power of their spell amid us is indeed that they have led me so far with a whole side of my plea for them still unspoken. This, however, I hope on another occasion to come back to; and I am caught meanwhile by my memory of how the note of this conviction was struck for me, with extraordinary force, many months ago and in the first flush of recognition of what the fate that had overtaken our earliest tides of arrival and appeal really meant—meant so that all fuller acquaintance, since pursued, has but piled one congruous reality after another upon the horror.

It was in September, in a tiny Sussex town which I had not quitted since the outbreak of the war, and where the advent of our first handful of fugitives before the warning of Louvain and Aerschoot and Termonde and Dinant had just been announced. Our small hill-top city, covering the steep sides of the compact pedestal crowned by its great church, had reserved a refuge at its highest point; and we had waited all day, from occasional train to train, for the moment at which we should attest our hospitality. It came at last, but late in the evening, when a vague outside rumour called me to my doorstep, where the unforgettable impression at once assaulted me. Up the precipitous little street that led from the station, over the old grass-grown cobbles where vehicles rarely pass, came the panting procession of the homeless and their comforting, their almost clinging entertainers, who seemed to hurry them on as in a sort of overflow of expression of the fever of charity. It was swift and eager, in the autumn darkness and under the flare of a single lamp—with no vociferation and, but for a woman's voice, scarce a sound save the shuffle of mounting feet and the thick-drawn breath of emotion. The note I except, however, was that of a young mother carrying her small child and surrounded by those who bore her on and on, almost lifting her as they went together. The resonance through our immemorial old street of her sobbing and sobbing cry was the voice itself of history; it brought home to me more things than I could then quite take the measure of, and these just because it expressed for her not direct anguish, but the incredibility, as who should say, of honest assured protection. Months have elapsed, and from having been then one of a few hundred she is now one of scores and scores of thousands: yet her cry is still in my ears, whether to speak most of what she had lately or of what she actually felt; and it plays, to my own sense, as a great fitful, tragic light over the dark exposure of her people.

THE AMERICAN VOLUNTEER MOTOR-AMBULANCE CORPS IN FRANCE

A Letter to the Editor of an American Journal

SIR,—Several of us Americans in London are so interested in the excellent work of this body, lately organised by Mr Richard Norton and now in active operation at the rear of a considerable part of the longest line of battle known to history, that I have undertaken to express to you our common conviction that our countrymen at home will share our interest and respond to such particulars as we are by this time able to give. The idea of the admirable enterprise was suggested to Mr Norton when, early in the course of the War, he saw at the American Hospital at Neuilly scores of cases of French and British wounded whose lives were lost, or who must incur life--long disability and suffering, through the long delay of their removal from the field of battle. To help energetically to remedy this dire fact struck him at once as possible, and his application of energy was so immediate and effective that in just three weeks after his return to London to take the work in hand he had been joined by a number of his countrymen and of others possessed of cars, who had offered them as ambulances already fitted or easily convertible, and had not less promptly offered themselves as capable chauffeurs. To this promptly gathered equipment, the recruiting of which no red tape had hampered and no postponement to committee-meetings had delayed, were at once added certain other cars of purchase—these made possible by funds rapidly received from many known and unknown friends in America. The fleet so collected amounted to some fifteen cars. To the service of the British Red Cross and that of the St John Ambulance it then addressed itself, gratefully welcomed, and enjoying from that moment the valuable association of Colonel A. J. Barry of the British Army, who was already employed in part on behalf of the Red Cross. I have within a few days had the opportunity to learn from this zealous and accomplished coadjutor, as well as from Mr Norton himself, some of the particulars of their comprehensive activity, they each having been able to dash over to London for a visit of the briefest duration. It has thus been brought home to me how much the success of the good work depends on American generosity both in the personal and the pecuniary way—exercised, that is, by the contribution of cars, to which personal service, that of their contributors, attaches itself, and of course by such gifts of money as shall make the Corps more and more worthy of its function and of the American name.

Its function is primarily that of gathering in the wounded, and those disabled by illness (though the question is almost always of the former,) from the *postes de secours* and the field hospitals, the various nearest points to the Front, bestrewn with patient victims, to which a motor-car can workably penetrate, and conveying them to the base hospitals, and when necessary the railway stations, from which they may be further directed upon places of care, centres of those possibilities of recovery which the splendid recent extension of surgical and medical science causes more and more to preponderate. The great and blessed fact is that conditions of recovery are largely secured by the promptitude and celerity that motor-transport offers, as compared with railway services at the mercy of constant interruption and arrest, in the case of bad and already neglected wounds, those aggravated by exposure and delay, the long lying on the poisonous field before the blest regimental *brancardiers* or stretcher-bearers, waiting for the shelter of night, but full also of their own strain of pluck, can come and remove them. Carried mostly by rude arts, a mercy much hindered at the best, to the shelter, often hastily improvised, at which first aid becomes possible for them, they are there, as immediately and tenderly as possible, stowed in our waiting or arriving cars, each of which receives as large a number as may be consistent with the particular suffering state of the stricken individual. Some of these are able to sit, at whatever cost from the inevitable shake over rough country roads; for others the lying posture only is thinkable, and the ideal car is the one which may humanely accommodate three men outstretched and four or five seated. Three outstretched is sometimes a tight fit, but when this is impossible the gain in poor *blessés assis* is the greater—wedged together though broken shoulder or smashed arm may have to be with a like shrinking and shuddering neighbour. The moral of these rigours is of course that the more numerous the rescuing vehicles the less inevitable the sore crowding. I find it difficult to express to you the sense of practical human pity, as well as the image of general helpful energy, applied in innumerable chance ways, that we get from the report of what the Corps has done, and holds itself in readiness to do, thanks to the admirable spirit of devotion without stint, of really passionate work, animating its individual members. These have been found beneficently and inexhaustibly active, it is interesting to be able to note, in proportion as they possess the general *educated* intelligence, the cultivated tradition of tact, and I may perhaps be allowed to confess that, for myself, I find a positive added beauty in the fact that the unpaid chauffeur, the wise amateur driver and ready lifter, helper, healer, and, so far as may be, consoler, is apt to be a University man and acquainted with other pursuits. One gets the sense that the labour, with its multiplied incidents and opportunities, is just unlimitedly inspiring to the keen spirit or the sympathetic soul, the recruit with energies and resources on hand that plead with him for the beauty of the vivid and palpable social result.

Not the least of the good offices open to our helpers are the odds and ends of aid determined by wayside encounters in a ravaged country, where distracted women and children flee from threatened or invaded villages, to be taken up, to be given the invaluable lift, if possible, in all the incoherence of their alarm and misery; sometimes with the elder men mixed in the tragic procession, tragi-comic even, very nearly, when the domestic or household objects they have snatched up in their headlong exodus, and are solemnly encumbered with, bear the oddest misproportion to the gravity of the case. They are hurried in, if the car be happily free, and carried on to comparative safety, but with the admirable cleverness and courage of the Frenchwoman of whatever class essentially in evidence in whatever contact; never more so, for instance, than when a rude field hospital has had of a sudden to be knocked together in the poor schoolhouse of a village, and the mangled and lacerated, brought into it on stretchers or on any rough handcart or trundled barrow that has been impressed into the service, have found the *villageoises*, bereft of their men, full of the bravest instinctive alertness, not wincing at sights of horror fit to try even trained sensibilities, handling shattered remnants of humanity with an art as extemporised as the refuge itself, and having each precarious charge ready for the expert transfer by the time the car has hurried up. Emphasised enough by the ceaseless thunder of the Front the quality of the French and the British resistance and the pitch of their spirit; but one feels what is meant none the less when one hears the variety of heroism and the brightness of devotion in the women over all the region of battle described from observation as unsurpassable. Do we take too much for granted in imagining that this offered intimacy of appreciation of such finest aspects of the admirable immortal France, and of a relation with them almost as illuminating to ourselves as beneficent to them, may itself rank as something of an appeal where the seeds of response to her magnificent struggle in the eye of our free longings and liberal impulses already exist?

I should mention that a particular great Army Corps, on the arrival of our first cars on the scene, appealed to them for all the service they could render, and that to this Corps they have been as yet uninterruptedly attached, on the condition of a reserve of freedom to respond at once to any British invitation to a transfer of activity. Such an assurance had already been given the Commissioner for the British Red Cross, on the part of Mr Norton and Colonel Barry, with their arrival at Boulogne, where that body cordially welcomed them, and whence in fact, on its request, a four-stretcher-car, with its American owner and another of our Volunteers in charge, proceeded to work for a fortnight, night and day, along the firing line on the Belgian frontier. Otherwise we have continuously enjoyed, in large, defined limits, up to the present writing, an association with one of the most tremendously engaged French Armies. The length of its line alone, were I to state it here in kilometres, would give some measure of the prodigious fighting stretch across what is practically the whole breadth of France, and it is in relation to a fraction of the former Front that we have worked. Very quickly, I may mention, we found one of our liveliest opportunities, Mr Norton and Colonel Barry proceeding together to ascertain what had become of one of the field hospitals known to have served in a small assaulted town a few days before, when, during a bombardment, Colonel Barry had saved many lives. Just as our Volunteers arrived a fresh bombardment began, and though assured by the fleeing inhabitants, including the mayor of the place, who was perhaps a trifle over-responsibly in advance of them, that there were no wounded left behind—as in fact proved to be the case—we nevertheless pushed on for full assurance. There were then no wounded to bring out, but it was our first happy chance of bearing away all the hopeless and helpless women and children we could carry. This was a less complicated matter, however, than that of one of Colonel Barry's particular reminiscences, an occasion when the Germans were advancing on a small place that it was clear they would take, and when pressing news came to him of 400 wounded in it, who were to be got out if humanly possible. They were got out and motored away—though it took the rescuing party thus three days, in the face of their difficulties and dangers, to effect the blest clearance. It may be imagined how precious in such conditions the power of the chauffeur-driven vehicle becomes, though indeed I believe the more special moral of this transaction, as given, was in the happy fact that the squad had blessedly been able to bring and keep with it four doctors, whose immediate service on the spot and during transport was the means of saving very many lives. The moral of that in turn would seem to be that the very ideal for the general case is the not so inconceivable volunteer who should be an ardent and gallant and not otherwise too much preoccupied young doctor with the possession of a car and the ability to drive it, above all the ability to offer it, as his crowning attribute. Perhaps I sketch in such terms a slightly fantastic figure, but there is so much of strenuous suggestion, which withal manages at the same time to be romantic, in the information before me, that it simply multiplies, for the hopeful mind, the possibilities and felicities of equipped good-will. An association of the grimmest reality clings at the same time, I am obliged to add, to the record of success I have just cited—the very last word of which seems to have been that in one of the houses of the little distracted town were two French Sisters of Mercy who were in charge of an old bedridden lady and whom, with the object of their care, every effort was made in vain to remove. They absolutely declined all such interference with the fate God had appointed them to meet as nuns—if it was His will to make them martyrs. The curtain drops upon what became of them, but they too illustrate in their way the range of the Frenchwoman's power to face the situation.

Still another form of high usefulness comes to our Corps, I should finally mention, in its opportunities for tracing the whereabouts and recovering the identity of the dead, the English dead, named in those grim lists, supplied to them by the military authorities, which their intercourse with the people in a given area where fighting has occurred enables them often blessedly to clear up. Their pervasiveness, their ubiquity, keeps them in touch with the people, witnesses of what happens on the battle-swept area when, after the storm has moved on, certain of the lifeless sweepings are gathered up. Old villagers, searched out and questioned, testify and give a clue through which the whereabouts of the committal to thin earth of the last mortality of this, that, or the other of the obscurely fallen comes as a kind of irony of relief to those waiting in suspense. This uncertainty had attached itself for weeks to the fate in particular of many of the men concerned in the already so historic retreat of the Allies from Mons—ground still considerably in the hands of the Germans, but also gradually accessible and where, as quickly as it becomes so, Colonel Barry pushes out into it in search of information. Sternly touching are such notes of general indication, information from the Curé, the village carpenter, the grave-digger of the place, a man called so-and-so and a gentleman called something else, as to the burial of forty-five dead English in the public cemetery of such and such a small locality, as to the interment somewhere else of 'an Englishman believed to be an officer,' as to a hundred English surprised in a certain church and killed all but forty, and buried, as is not always their fortune for their kindred, without removal of their discs of identification. Among such like data we move when not among those of a more immediate violence, and all to be in their way scarce less considerately handled. Mixed with such gleanings one comes upon other matters of testimony of which one hopes equal note is made—testimony as to ferocities perpetrated upon the civil population which I may not here specify. Every form of assistance and inquiry takes place of course in conditions of some danger, thanks to the risk of stray bullets and shells, not infrequently met when cars operate, as they neither avoid doing nor wastefully seek to do, in proximity to the lines. The Germans, moreover, are noted as taking the view that the insignia of the Red Cross, with the implication of the precarious freight it covers, are in all circumstances a good mark for their shots; a view characteristic of their belligerent system at large, but not more deterrent for the ministers of the adversary in this connection than in any other, when the admirable end is in question.

I have doubtless said enough, however, in illustration of the interest attaching to all this service, a service in which not one of the forces of social energy and devotion, not one of the true social qualities, sympathy, ingenuity, tact, and taste, fail to come into play. Such an exercise of them, as all the incidental possibilities are taken advantage of, represents for us all, who are happily not engaged in the huge destructive work, the play not simply of a reparatory or consolatory, but a positively productive and creative virtue in which there is a peculiar honour. We Americans are as little neutrals as possible where any aptitude for any action, of whatever kind, that affirms life and freshly and inventively exemplifies it, instead of overwhelming and undermining it, is concerned. Great is the chance, in fact, for exhibiting this as our entirely elastic, our supremely characteristic, social aptitude. We cannot do so cheaply, indeed, any more than the opposite course is found, under whatever fatuity of presumption, inexpensive and ready-made. What I therefore invite all those whom this notice may reach to understand, as for that matter they easily will, is that the expenses of our enlightened enterprise have to be continuously met, and that if it has confidence in such support it may go on in all the alert pride and pity that need be desired. I am assured that the only criticism the members of the Corps make of it is that they wish more of their friends would come and support it either personally or financially—or, best of all, of course, both. At the moment I write I learn this invocation to have been met to the extent of Mr Norton's having within two or three days annexed five fresh cars, with their owners to work them—and all, as I hear it put with elation, 'excellent University men.' As an extremely helpful factor on the part of Volunteers is some facility in French and the goodwill to stay on for whatever reasonable length of time, I assume the excellence of these gentlemen to include those signal merits. Most members of the Staff of thirty-four in all (as the number till lately at least has stood) have been glad to pay their own living expenses; but it is taken for granted that in cases where individuals are unable to meet that outlay indefinitely the subscribers to the Fund will not grudge its undertaking to find any valuable man in food and lodging. Such charges amount at the outside to 1 dollar 75 per day. The expenses of petrol and tyres are paid by the French Government or the British Red Cross, so that the contributor of the car is at costs only for the maintenance of his chauffeur, if he brings one, or for necessary repairs. Mr Eliot Norton, of 2 Rector Street, New York, is our recipient of donations on your side of the sea, Mr George F. Read, Hon. Treas., care of Messrs Brown, Shipley & Co., 123 Pall Mall, S.W., kindly performs this office in London, and I am faithfully yours,

HENRY JAMES.

LONDON, *November 25, 1914.*

FRANCE

I THINK that if there is a general ground in the world, on which an appeal might be made, in a civilised circle, with a sense of its being uttered only to meet at once and beyond the need of insistence a certain supreme recognition and response, the idea of what France and the French mean to the educated spirit of man would be the nameable thing. It would be the cause uniting us most quickly in an act of glad intelligence, uniting us with the least need of any wondering why. We should understand and answer together just by the magic of the mention, the touch of the two or three words, and this in proportion to our feeling ourselves social and communicating creatures—to the point, in fact, of a sort of shame at any imputation of our not liberally understanding, of our waiting in any degree to be nudged or hustled. The case of France, as one may hold it, where the perceptive social mind is concerned and set in motion, is thus only to be called exquisite—so far as we don't seem so to qualify things *down*. We certainly all feel, in the beautiful connection, in two general ways; one of these being that the spring pressed with such happy effect lifts the sense by its mere vibration into the lightest and brightest air in which, taking our world all round, it is given to our finer interest about things to breathe and move; and the other being that just having our intelligence, our experience at its freest and bravest, taken for granted, is a compliment to us, as not purely instinctive persons, which we should miss, if it were not paid, rather to the degree of finding the omission an insult.

Such, as I say, is our easy relation to the sound of a voice raised, even however allusively and casually, on behalf of that great national and social presence which has always most oppositely, most sensibly, most obsessively, as I surely may put it, and above all most dazzlingly, neighboured and admonished us here: after such a fashion as really to have made the felt breath of its life, across an interval constantly narrowing, a part of our education as distinguished from our luck. Our luck in all our past has been enormous, the greatest luck on the whole, assuredly, that any race has ever had; but it has never been a conscious reaction or a gathered fruition, as one may say; it has just been a singular felicity of position and of temperament, and this felicity has made us observe and perceive and reflect much less than it has made us directly act and profit and enjoy: enjoy of course by attending tremendously to all the business involved in our position. So far as we have had reactions, therefore, they have not sprung, when they have been at all intensified, from the extraordinary good fortune of our state. Unless indeed I may put it that what they *have* very considerably sprung from has been exactly a part of our general prodigy—the good fortune itself of our being neighboured by a native genius so different from our own, so suggestive of wondrous and attaching comparisons, as to keep us chronically aware of the difference and the contrast and yet all the while help us to see into them and through them.

We were not, to all appearance, appointed by fate for the most perceptive and penetrative offices conceivable; so that to have over against us and within range a proposition, as we nowadays say, that could only grow more and more vivid, more and more engaging and inspiring, in the measure of our growth of criticism and curiosity, or, in other words, of the capacity just to pay attention, pay attention otherwise than by either sticking very fast at home or inquiring of the Antipodes, the Antipodes almost exclusively—what has that practically been for us but one of the very choicest phases of our luck aforesaid, one of the most appraisable of our felicities? the very one, doubtless, that our dissimilarity of temperament and taste would have most contradictiously and most correctively prescribed from the moment we were not to be left simply to stew in our juice! If the advantage I so characterise was to be in its own way thoroughly affirmative, there was yet nothing about it to do real or injurious violence to that abysmal good nature which sometimes strikes me as our most effective contribution to human history. The vision of France, at any rate, so close and so clear at propitious hours, was to grow happily illustrational for us as nothing else in any like relation to us could possibly have become. Other families have a way, on good opportunity, of interesting us more than our own, and here was this immense acquaintance extraordinarily mattering for us and at the same time not irritating us by a single claim of cousinship or a single liberty taken on any such score. Any liberties taken were much rather liberties, I think, of ours—always abounding as we did in quite free, and perhaps slightly rough, and on the whole rather superficial, movement beyond our island circle and toward whatever lay in our path. France lay very much in our path, our path to almost everything that could beckon us forth from our base—and there were very few things in the world or places on the globe that didn't so beckon us; according to which she helped us along on our expansive course a good deal more, doubtless, than either she or we always knew.

All of which, you see, is but a manner of making my point that her name means more than anything in the world to us but just our own. Only at present it means ever so much more, almost unspeakably more, than it has ever done in the past, and I can't help inviting you to feel with me, for a very few moments, what the real force of this association to which we now throb consists of, and why it so moves us. We enjoy generous emotions *because* they are generous, because generosity is a noble passion and a glow, because we spring with it for the time above our common pedestrian pace—and this just in proportion as all questions and doubts about it drop to the ground. But great reasons never spoil a great sympathy, and to see an inspiring object in a strong light never made any such a shade less inspiring. So, therefore, in these days when our great neighbour and Ally is before us in a beauty that is tragic, tragic because menaced and overdarkened, the closest possible appreciation of what it is that is thereby in peril for ourselves and for the world makes the image shine with its highest brightness at the same time that the cloud upon it is made more black. When I sound the depth of my own affection so fondly excited, I take the like measure for all of us and feel the glad recognition I meet in thus putting it to you, for our full illumination, that what happens to France happens to all that part of ourselves which we are most proud, and most finely advised, to enlarge and cultivate and consecrate.

Our heroic friend sums up for us, in other words, and has always summed up, the life of the mind and the life of the senses alike, taken together, in the most irrepressible freedom of either—and, after that fashion, positively lives *for* us, carries on experience for us; does it under our tacit and our at present utterly ungrudging view of her being formed and endowed and constantly prompted, toward such doing, on all sorts of sides that are simply so many reasons for our standing off, standing off in a sort of awed intellectual hush or social suspense, and watching and admiring and thanking her. She is sole and single in this, that she takes charge of those of the interests of man which most dispose him to fraternise with himself, to pervade all his possibilities and to taste all his faculties, and in consequence to find and to make the earth a friendlier, an easier, and especially a more various sojourn; and the great thing is the amiability and the authority, intimately combined, with which she has induced us all to trust her on this ground. There are matters as to which every set of people has of course most to trust itself, most to feel its own genius and its own stoutness—as we are here and all round about us knowing and abiding by that now as we have never done. But I verily think there has never been anything in the world—since the most golden aspect of antiquity at least—like the way in which France has been trusted to gather the rarest and fairest and sweetest fruits of our so tremendously and so mercilessly turned-up garden of life. She has gardened where the soil of humanity has been most grateful and the aspect, so to call it, most toward the sun, and there, at the high and yet mild and fortunate centre, she has grown the precious, intimate, the nourishing, finishing things that she has inexhaustibly scattered abroad. And if we have all so taken them from her, so expected them from her as our right, to the point that she would have seemed positively to fail of a passed pledge to help us to happiness if she had disappointed us, this has been because of her treating us to the impression of genius as no nation since the Greeks has treated the watching world, and because of our feeling that genius at that intensity is infallible.

What it has all amounted to, as I say, is that we have never known otherwise an agent so beautifully organised, organised from within, for a mission, and that such an organisation at free play has made us really want never to lift a finger to break the charm. We catch at every turn of our present long-drawn crisis indeed that portentous name: it's displayed to us on a measureless scale that our Enemy is organised, organised possibly to the effect of binding us with a spell if anything *could* keep us passive. The term has been in a manner, by that association, compromised and vulgarised: I say vulgarised because any history of organisation from without and for intended aggression and self-imposition, however elaborate the thing may be, shows for merely mechanical and bristling compared with the condition of being naturally and functionally endowed and appointed. This last is the only fair account of the complete and perfect case that France has shown us and that civilisation has depended on for half its assurances. Well, now, we have before us this boundless extension of the case, that, as we have always known what it was to see the wonderful character I speak of range through its variety and keep shining with another and still another light, so in these days we assist at what we may verily call the supreme evidence of its incomparable gift for vivid exhibition. It takes our great Ally, and her only, to be as vivid for concentration, for reflection, for intelligent, inspired contraction of life toward an end all but smothered in sacrifice, as she has ever been for the most splendidly wasteful diffusion and communication; and to give us a view of her nature and her mind in which, laying down almost every advantage, every art and every appeal that we have generally known her by, she takes on energies, forms of collective sincerity, silent eloquence and selected example that are fresh revelations—and so, bleeding at every pore, while at no time in all her history so completely erect, makes us feel her perhaps as never before our incalculable, immortal France.

THE LONG WARDS

THERE comes back to me out of the distant past an impression of the citizen soldier at once in his collective grouping and in his impaired, his more or less war-worn state, which was to serve me for long years as the most intimate vision of him that my span of life was likely to disclose. This was a limited affair indeed, I recognise as I try to recover it, but I mention it because I was to find at the end of time that I had kept it in reserve, left it lurking deep down in my sense of things, however shyly and dimly, however confusedly even, as a term of comparison, a glimpse of something by the loss of which I should have been the poorer; such a residuary possession of the spirit, in fine, as only needed darkness to close round it a little from without in order to give forth a vague phosphorescent light. It was early, it must have been very early, in our Civil War; yet not so early but that a large number of those who had answered President Lincoln's first call for an army had had time to put in their short period (the first term was so short then, as was likewise the first number,) and reappear again in camp, one of those of their small New England state, under what seemed to me at the hour, that of a splendid autumn afternoon, the thickest mantle of heroic history. If I speak of the impression as confused I certainly justify that mark of it by my failure to be clear at this moment as to how much they were in general the worse for wear—since they can't have been exhibited to me, through their waterside settlement of tents and improvised shanties, in anything like hospital conditions. However, I cherish the rich ambiguity, and have always cherished it, for the sake alone of the general note exhaled, the thing that has most kept remembrance unbroken. I carried away from the place the impression, the one that not only was never to fade, but was to show itself susceptible of extraordinary eventual enrichment. I may not pretend now to refer it to the more particular sources it drew upon at that summer's end of 1861, or to say why my repatriated warriors were, if not somehow definitely stricken, so largely either lying in apparent helplessness or moving about in confessed languor: it suffices me that I have always thought of them as expressing themselves at almost every point in the minor key, and that this has been the reason of their interest. What I call the note therefore is the characteristic the most of the essence and the most inspiring—inspiring I mean for consideration of the admirable sincerity that we thus catch in the act: the note of the quite abysmal softness, the exemplary genius for accommodation, that forms the alternative aspect, the passive as distinguished from the active, of the fighting man whose business is in the first instance formidably to bristle. This aspect has been produced, I of course recognise, amid the horrors that the German powers had, up to a twelvemonth ago, been for years conspiring to let loose upon the world by such appalling engines and agencies as mankind had never before dreamed of; but just that is the lively interest of the fact unfolded to us now on a scale beside which, and though save indeed for a single restriction, the whole previous illustration of history turns pale. Even if I catch but in a generalising blur that exhibition of the first American levies as a measure of experience had stamped and harrowed them, the signally attaching mark that I refer to is what I most recall; so that if I didn't fear, for the connection, to appear to compare the slighter things with the so much greater, the diminished shadow with the far-spread substance, I should speak of my small old scrap of truth, miserably small in contrast with the immense evidence even then to have been gathered, but in respect to which latter occasion didn't come to me, as having contained possibilities of development that I must have languished well-nigh during a lifetime to crown it with.

One had during the long interval not lacked opportunity for a vision of the soldier at peace, moving to and fro with a professional eye on the horizon, but not fished out of the bloody welter and laid down to pant, as we actually see him among the Allies, almost on the very bank and within sound and sight of his deepest element. The effect of many of the elapsing years, the time in England and France and Italy, had indeed been to work his collective presence so closely and familiarly into any human scene pretending to a full illustration of our most generally approved conditions that I confess to having missed him rather distressfully from the picture of things offered me during a series of months spent not long ago in a few American cities after years of disconnection. I can scarce say why I missed him sadly rather than gladly—I might so easily have prefigured one's delight in his absence; but certain it

43

is that my almost outraged consciousness of our practically doing without him amid American conditions was a revelation of the degree in which his great imaging, his great reminding and enhancing function is rooted in the European basis. I felt his non-existence on the American positively produce a void which nothing else, as a vivifying substitute, hurried forward to fill; this being indeed the case with many of the other voids, the most aching, which left the habituated eye to cast about as for something to nibble in a state of dearth. We never know, I think, how much these wanting elements have to suggest to the pampered mind till we feel it living in view of the community from which they have been simplified away. On these occasions they conspire with the effect of certain other, certain similar expressions, examples of social life proceeding as by the serene, the possibly too serene, process of mere ignorance, to bring to a head for the fond observer the wonder of what is supposed to strike, for the projection of a finished world, the note that they are not there to strike. However, as I quite grant the hypothesis of an observer still fond and yet remarking the lapse of the purple patch of militarism but with a joy unclouded, I limit myself to the merely personal point that the fancy of a particular brooding analyst *could* so sharply suffer from a vagueness of privation, something like an unseasoned observational diet, and then, rather to his relief, find the mystery cleared up. And the strict relevancy of the bewilderment I glance at, moreover, becomes questionable, further, by reason of my having, with the outbreak of the horrors in which we are actually steeped, caught myself staring at the exhibited militarism of the general British scene not much less ruefully than I could remember to have stared, a little before, at the utter American deficit. Which proves after all that the rigour of the case had begun at a bound to defy the largest luxury of thought; so that the presence of the military in the picture on the mere moderate insular scale struck one as 'furnishing' a menaced order but in a pitiful and pathetic degree.

The degree was to alter, however, by swift shades, just as one's comprehension of the change grew and grew with it; and thus it was that, to cut short the record of our steps and stages, we have left immeasurably behind us here the question of what might or what should have been. That belonged, with whatever beguiled or amused ways of looking at it, to the abyss of our past delusion, a collective state of mind in which it had literally been possible to certain sophists to argue that, so far from not having soldiers enough, we had more than we were likely to know any respectable public call for. It was in the very fewest weeks that we replaced a pettifogging consciousness by the most splendidly liberal, and, having swept through all the first phases of anxiety and suspense, found no small part of our measure of the matter settle down to an almost luxurious study of our multiplied defenders after the fact, as I may call it, or in the light of that acquaintance with them as products supremely tried and tested which I began by speaking of. We were up to our necks in this relation before we could turn round, and what upwards of a year's experience of it has done in the contributive and enriching way may now well be imagined. I might feel that my marked generalisation, the main hospital impression, steeps the case in too strong or too stupid a synthesis, were it not that to consult my memory, a recollection of countless associative contacts, is to see the emphasis almost absurdly thrown on my quasi-paradox. Just so it is of singular interest for the witnessing mind itself to feel the happy truth stoutly resist any qualifying hint—since I am so struck with the charm, as I can only call it, of the tone and temper of the man of action, the creature appointed to advance and explode and destroy, and elaborately instructed as to how to do these things, reduced to helplessness in the innumerable instances now surrounding us. It doesn't in the least take the edge from my impression that his sweet reasonableness, representing the opposite end of his wondrous scale, is probably the very oldest story of the touching kind in the world; so far indeed from my claiming the least originality for the appealing appearance as it has lately reached me from so many sides, I find its suggestion of vast communities, communities of patience and placidity, acceptance and submission pushed to the last point, to be just what makes the whole show most illumination.

'Wonderful that, from east to west, they must *all* be like this,' one says to oneself in presence of certain consistencies, certain positive monotonies of aspect; 'wonderful that if joy of battle (for the classic term, in spite of new horrors, seems clearly still to keep its old sense,) has, to so attested a pitch, animated these forms, the disconnection of spirit should be so prompt and complete, should hand the creature over as by the easiest turn to the last refinements of accommodation. The disconnection of the flesh, of physical function in whatever ravaged area, *that* may well be measureless; but how interesting, if the futility of such praise doesn't too much dishonour the subject, the exquisite anomaly of the intimate readjustment of the really more inflamed and exasperated part, or in other words of the imagination, the captured, the haunted vision, to life at its most innocent and most ordered!' To that point one's unvarying thought of the matter, which yet, though but a meditation without a conclusion, becomes the very air in which fond attention spends itself. So far as commerce of the acceptable, the tentatively helpful kind goes, one looks for the key to success then, among the victims, exactly on that ground of the apprehension pacified and almost, so to call it, trivialised. The attaching thing becomes thus one's intercourse with the imagination of the particular patient subject, the individual himself, in the measure in which this interest bears us up and carries us along; which name for the life of his spirit has to cover, by a considerable stretch, all the ground. By the stretch of the name, moreover, I am far from meaning any stretch of the faculty itself—which remains for the most part a considerably contracted or inert force, a force in fact often so undeveloped as to be insusceptible of measurement at all, so that one has to resort, in face of the happy fact that communion still does hold good, to some other descriptive sign for it. That sign, however, fortunately presents itself with inordinate promptitude and fits to its innocent head with the last perfection the cap, in fact the very crown, of an office that we can only appraise as predetermined good nature. We after this fashion score our very highest on behalf of a conclusion, I think, in feeling that whether or no the British warrior's good nature has much range of fancy, his imagination, whatever there may be of it, is at least so good-natured as to show absolutely everything it touches, everything without exception, even the worst machinations of the enemy, in that colour. Variety and diversity of exhibition, in a world virtually divided as now into hospitals and the preparation of subjects for them, are, I accordingly conceive, to be looked for quite away from the question of physical patience, of the general consent to suffering and mutilation, and, instead of that, in this connection of the sort of mind and thought, the sort of moral attitude, that are born of the sufferer's other relations; which I like to think of as being different from country to country, from class to class, and as having their fullest national and circumstantial play.

It would be of the essence of these remarks, could I give them within my space all the particular applications naturally awaiting them, that they pretend to refer here to the British private soldier only—generalisation about his officers would take us so considerably further and so much enlarge our view. The high average of the beauty and modesty of these, in the stricken state, causes them to affect me, I frankly confess, as probably the very flower of the human race. One's apprehension of 'Tommy'—and I scarce know whether more to dislike the liberty this mode of reference takes with him, or to incline to retain it for the tenderness really latent in it—is in itself a theme for fine notation, but it has brought me thus only to the door of the boundless hospital ward in which, these many months, I have seen the successive and the so strangely quiet tides of his presence ebb and flow, and it stays me there before the incalculable vista. The perspective stretches away, in its mild order, after the fashion of a tunnel boring into the very character of the people, and so going on for ever—never arriving or coming out, that is, at anything in the nature of a station, a junction or a terminus. So it draws off through the infinite of the common personal life, but planted and bordered, all along its passage, with the thick-growing flower of the individual illustration, this sometimes vivid enough and sometimes pathetically pale. The great fact, to my now so informed vision, is that it undiscourageably continues and that an unceasing repetition of its testifying particulars seems never either to exhaust its sense or to satisfy that of the beholder. Its sense, indeed, if I may so far simplify, is pretty well always the same, that of the jolly fatalism above-mentioned, a state of moral hospitality to the practices of fortune, however outrageous, that may at times fairly be felt as providing amusement, providing a new and thereby a refreshing turn of the personal situation, for the most interested party. It is true that one may be sometimes moved to wonder which is the most interested party, the stricken subject in his numbered bed or the friendly, the unsated inquirer who has tried to forearm himself against such a measure of the 'criticism of life' as might well be expected to break upon him from the couch in question, and who yet, a thousand occasions for it having been, all round him, inevitably neglected, finds this ingenious provision quite left on his hands. He may well ask himself what he is to do with people who so consistently and so comfortably content themselves with *being*—being for the most part incuriously and instinctively admirable—that nothing whatever is left of them for reflection as distinguished from their own practice; but the only answer that comes is the reproduction of the note. He may, in the interest of appreciation, try the experiment of lending them some scrap of a complaint or a curse in order that they shall meet him on congruous ground, the ground of encouragement to his own participating impulse. They are imaged, under that possibility, after the manner of those unfortunates, the very poor, the victims of a fire or shipwreck, to whom you have to lend something to wear before they can come to thank you for helping them. The inmates of the long wards, however, have no use for any imputed or derivative sentiments or reasons; they feel in their own way, they feel a great deal, they don't at all conceal from you that to have seen what they have seen is to have seen things horrible and monstrous—but there is no estimate of them for which they seek to be indebted to you, and nothing they less invite from you than to show them that such visions must have poisoned their world. Their world isn't in the least poisoned; they have assimilated their experience by a process scarce at all to be distinguished from their having healthily got rid of it.

The case thus becomes for you that they consist wholly of their applied virtue, which is accompanied with no waste of consciousness whatever. The virtue may strike you as having been, and as still being, greater in some examples than in others, but it has throughout the same sign of differing at almost no point from a supreme amiability. How can creatures so amiable, you allow yourself vaguely to wonder, have welcomed even for five minutes the stress of carnage? and how can the stress of carnage, the murderous impulse at the highest pitch, have left so little distortion of the moral nature? It has left none at all that one has at the end of many months been able to discover; so that perhaps the most steadying and refreshing effect of intercourse with these hospital friends is through the almost complete rest from the facing of generalisations to which it treats you. One would even like, perhaps, as a stimulus to talk, more generalisation; but one gets enough of that out in the world, and one doesn't get there nearly so much of what one gets in this perspective, the particular perfect sufficiency of the extraordinary principle, whatever it is, which makes the practical answer so supersede any question or any argument that it seems fairly to have acted by chronic instinctive anticipation, the habit of freely throwing the personal weight into any obvious opening. The personal weight, in its various forms and degrees, is what lies there with a head on the pillow and whatever wise bandages thereabout or elsewhere, and it becomes interesting in itself, and just in proportion, I think, to its having had all its history after the fact. All its history is that of the particular application which has brought it to the pass at which you find it, and is a stream round about which you have to press a little hard to make it flow clear. Then, in many a case, it does flow, certainly, as clear as one could wish, and with the strain that it is always somehow English history and illustrates afresh the English way of doing things and regarding them, of feeling and naming them. The sketch extracted is apt to be least coloured when the prostrate historian, as I may call him, is an Englishman of the English; it has more point, though not perhaps more essential tone, when he is a Scot of the Scots, and has most when he is an Irishman of the Irish; but there is absolutely no difference, in the light of race and save as by inevitable variation from individual to individual, about the really constant and precious matter, the attested possession on the part of the contributor of a free loose undisciplined quantity of being to contribute.

This is the palpable and ponderable, the admirably appreciable, residuum—as to which if I be asked just how it is that I pluck the flower of amiability from the bramble of an individualism so bristling with accents, I am afraid I can only say that the accents would seem by the mercy of chance to fall together in the very sense that permits us to detach the rose with the fewest scratches. The rose of active good nature, irreducible, incurable, or in other words all irreflective, *that* is the variety which the individualistic tradition happens, up and down these islands, to wear upon its ample breast— even it may be with considerable effect of monotony. There it is, for what it is, and the very simplest summary of one's poor bedside practice is perhaps to confess that one has most of all kept one's nose buried in it. There hangs about the poor practitioner by that fact, I profess, an aroma not doubtless at all mixed or in the least mystical, but so unpervertedly wholesome that what can I pronounce it with any sort of conscience but sweet? That is the rough, unless I rather say the smooth, report of it; which covers of course, I hasten to add, a constant shift of impression within the happy limits. Did I not, by way of introduction to these awaiters of acknowledgment, find myself first of all, early in the autumn, in presence of the first aligned rows of lacerated Belgians?—the eloquence of whose mere mute expression of their state, and thereby of their cause, remains to me a vision unforgettable for ever, and this even though I may not here stretch my scale to make them, Flemings of Flanders though they were, fit into my remarks with the English of the English and the Scotch of the Scotch. If other witnesses might indeed here fit in they would decidedly come nearest, for there were aspects under which one might almost have taken them simply for Britons comparatively starved of sport and, to make up for that, on straighter and homelier terms with their other senses and appetites. But their effect, thanks to their being so seated in everything that their ripe and rounded temperament had done for them, was to make their English entertainers, and their successors in the long wards especially, seem ever so much more complicated—besides making of what had happened to themselves, for that matter, an enormity of outrage beyond all thought and pity. Their fate had cut into their spirit to a peculiar degree through their flesh, as if they had had an unusual thickness of this, so to speak—which up to that time had protected while it now but the more exposed and, collectively, entrapped them; so that the ravaged and plundered domesticity that one felt in them, which was mainly what they had to oppose, made the terms of their exile and their suffering an extension of the possible and the dreadful. But all that vision is a chapter by itself—the essence of which is perhaps that it has been the privilege of this placid and sturdy people to show the world a new shade and measure of the tragic and the horrific. The first wash of the great Flemish tide ebbed at any rate from the hospitals— creating moreover the vast needs that were to be so unprecedentedly met, and the native procession which has prompted these remarks set steadily in. I have played too uncertain a light, I am well aware, not arresting it at half the possible points, yet with one aspect of the case staring out so straight as to form the vivid moral that asks to be drawn. The deepest impression from the sore human stuff with which such observation deals is that of its being strong and sound in an extraordinary degree for the conditions producing it. These conditions represent, one feels at the best, the crude and the waste, the ignored and neglected state; and under the sense of the small care and scant provision that have attended such hearty and happy growths, struggling into life and air with no furtherance to speak of, the question comes pressingly home of what a better economy might, or verily mightn't, result in. If this abundance all slighted and unencouraged can still comfort us, what wouldn't it do for us tended and fostered and cultivated? That is my moral, for I believe in Culture—speaking strictly now of the honest and of our own congruous kind.

About Author

Henry James OM (15 April 1843 – 28 February 1916) was an American-British author regarded as a key transitional figure between literary realism and literary modernism, and is considered by many to be among the greatest novelists in the English language. He was the son of Henry James Sr. and the brother of renowned philosopher and psychologist William James and diarist Alice James.

He is best known for a number of novels dealing with the social and marital interplay between émigré Americans, English people, and continental Europeans. Examples of such novels include The Portrait of a Lady, The Ambassadors, and The Wings of the Dove. His later works were increasingly experimental. In describing the internal states of mind and social dynamics of his characters, James often made use of a style in which ambiguous or contradictory motives and impressions were overlaid or juxtaposed in the discussion of a character's psyche. For their unique ambiguity, as well as for other aspects of their composition, his late works have been compared to impressionist painting.

His novella The Turn of the Screw has garnered a reputation as the most analysed and ambiguous ghost story in the English language and remains his most widely adapted work in other media. He also wrote a number of other highly regarded ghost stories and is considered one of the greatest masters of the field.

James published articles and books of criticism, travel, biography, autobiography, and plays. Born in the United States, James largely relocated to Europe as a young man and eventually settled in England, becoming a British subject in 1915, one year before his death. James was nominated for the Nobel Prize in Literature in 1911, 1912 and 1916.

Life

Early years, 1843–1883

James was born at 2 Washington Place in New York City on 15 April 1843. His parents were Mary Walsh and Henry James Sr. His father was intelligent and steadfastly congenial. He was a lecturer and philosopher who had inherited independent means from his father, an Albany banker and investor. Mary came from a wealthy family long settled in New York City. Her sister Katherine lived with her adult family for an extended period of time. Henry Jr. had three brothers, William, who was one year his senior, and younger brothers Wilkinson (Wilkie) and Robertson. His younger sister was Alice. Both of his parents were of Irish and Scottish descent.

The family first lived in Albany, at 70 N. Pearl St., and then moved to Fourteenth Street in New York City when James was still a young boy. His education was calculated by his father to expose him to many influences, primarily scientific and philosophical; it was described by Percy Lubbock, the editor of his selected letters, as "extraordinarily haphazard and promiscuous." James did not share the usual education in Latin and Greek classics. Between 1855 and 1860, the James' household traveled to London, Paris, Geneva, Boulogne-sur-Mer and Newport, Rhode Island, according to the father's current interests and publishing ventures, retreating to the United States when funds were low. Henry studied primarily with tutors and briefly attended schools while the family traveled in Europe. Their longest stays were in France, where Henry began to feel at home and became fluent in French. He was afflicted with a stutter, which seems to have manifested itself only when he spoke English; in French, he did not stutter.

In 1860 the family returned to Newport. There Henry became a friend of the painter John La Farge, who introduced him to French literature, and in particular, to Balzac. James later called Balzac his "greatest master," and said that he had learned more about the craft of fiction from him than from anyone else.

In the autumn of 1861 Henry received an injury, probably to his back, while fighting a fire. This injury, which resurfaced at times throughout his life, made him unfit for military service in the American Civil War.

In 1864 the James family moved to Boston, Massachusetts to be near William, who had enrolled first in the Lawrence Scientific School at Harvard and then in the medical school. In 1862 Henry attended Harvard Law School, but realised that he was not interested in studying law. He pursued his interest in literature and associated with authors and critics William Dean Howells and Charles Eliot Norton in Boston and Cambridge, formed lifelong friendships with Oliver Wendell Holmes Jr., the future Supreme Court Justice, and with James and Annie Fields, his first professional mentors.

His first published work was a review of a stage performance, "Miss Maggie Mitchell in Fanchon the Cricket," published in 1863. About a year later, A Tragedy of Error, his first short story, was published anonymously. James's first payment was for an appreciation of Sir Walter Scott's novels, written for the North American Review. He wrote fiction and non-fiction pieces for The Nation and Atlantic Monthly, where Fields was editor. In 1871 he published his first novel, Watch and Ward, in serial form in the Atlantic Monthly. The novel was later published in book form in 1878.

During a 14-month trip through Europe in 1869–70 he met Ruskin, Dickens, Matthew Arnold, William Morris, and George Eliot. Rome impressed him profoundly. "Here I am then in the Eternal City," he wrote to his brother William. "At last—for the first time—I live!" He attempted to support himself as a freelance writer in Rome, then secured a position as Paris correspondent for the New York Tribune, through the influence of its editor John Hay. When these efforts failed he returned to New York City. During 1874 and 1875 he published Transatlantic Sketches, A Passionate Pilgrim, and Roderick Hudson. During this early period in his career he was influenced by Nathaniel Hawthorne.

In 1869 he settled in London. There he established relationships with Macmillan and other publishers, who paid for serial installments that they would later publish in book form. The audience for these serialized novels was largely made up of middle-class women, and James struggled to fashion serious literary work within the strictures imposed by editors' and publishers' notions of what was suitable for young women to read. He lived in rented rooms but was able to join gentlemen's clubs that had libraries and where he could entertain male friends. He was introduced to English society by Henry Adams and Charles Milnes Gaskell, the latter introducing him to the Travellers' and the Reform Clubs.

In the fall of 1875 he moved to the Latin Quarter of Paris. Aside from two trips to America, he spent the next three decades—the rest of his life—in Europe. In Paris he met Zola, Alphonse Daudet, Maupassant, Turgenev, and others. He stayed in Paris only a year before moving to London.

In England he met the leading figures of politics and culture. He continued to be a prolific writer, producing The American (1877), The Europeans (1878), a revision of Watch and Ward (1878), French Poets and Novelists (1878), Hawthorne (1879), and several shorter works of fiction. In 1878 Daisy Miller established his fame on both sides of the Atlantic. It drew notice perhaps mostly because it depicted a woman whose behavior is outside the social norms of Europe. He also began his first masterpiece, The Portrait of a Lady, which would appear in 1881.

In 1877 he first visited Wenlock Abbey in Shropshire, home of his friend Charles Milnes Gaskell whom he had met through Henry Adams. He was much inspired by the darkly romantic Abbey and the surrounding countryside, which features in his essay Abbeys and Castles. In particular the gloomy monastic fishponds behind the Abbey are said to have inspired the lake in The Turn of the Screw.

While living in London, James continued to follow the careers of the "French realists", Émile Zola in particular. Their stylistic methods influenced his own work in the years to come. Hawthorne's influence on him faded during this period, replaced by George Eliot and Ivan Turgenev. 1879–1882 saw the publication of The Europeans, Washington Square, Confidence, and The Portrait of a Lady. He visited America in 1882–1883, then returned to London.

The period from 1881 to 1883 was marked by several losses. His mother died in 1881, followed by his father a few months later, and then by his brother Wilkie. Emerson, an old family friend, died in 1882. His friend Turgenev died in 1883.

Middle years, 1884–1897

In 1884 James made another visit to Paris. There he met again with Zola, Daudet, and Goncourt. He had been following the careers of the French "realist" or "naturalist" writers, and was increasingly influenced by them. In 1886, he published The Bostonians and The Princess Casamassima, both influenced by the French writers he'd studied assiduously. Critical reaction and sales were poor. He wrote to Howells that the books had hurt his career rather than helped because they had "reduced the desire, and demand, for my productions to zero". During this time he became friends with Robert Louis Stevenson, John Singer Sargent, Edmund Gosse, George du Maurier, Paul Bourget, and Constance Fenimore Woolson. His third novel from the 1880s was The Tragic Muse. Although he was following the precepts of Zola in his novels of the '80s, their tone and attitude are closer to the fiction of Alphonse Daudet. The lack of critical and financial success for his novels during this period led him to try writing for the theatre. (His dramatic works and his experiences with theatre are discussed below.)

In the last quarter of 1889, he started translating "for pure and copious lucre" Port Tarascon, the third volume of Alphonse Daudet adventures of Tartarin de Tarascon. Serialized in Harper's Monthly Magazine from June 1890, this translation praised as "clever" by The Spectator was published in January 1891 by Sampson Low, Marston, Searle & Rivington.

After the stage failure of Guy Domville in 1895, James was near despair and thoughts of death plagued him. The years spent on dramatic works were not entirely a loss. As he moved into the last phase of his career he found ways to adapt dramatic techniques into the novel form.

In the late 1880s and throughout the 1890s James made several trips through Europe. He spent a long stay in Italy in 1887. In that year the short novel The Aspern Papers and The Reverberator were published.

Late years, 1898–1916

In 1897–1898 he moved to Rye, Sussex, and wrote The Turn of the Screw. 1899–1900 saw the publication of The Awkward Age and The Sacred

Fount. During 1902–1904 he wrote The Ambassadors, The Wings of the Dove, and The Golden Bowl.

In 1904 he revisited America and lectured on Balzac. In 1906–1910 he published The American Scene and edited the "New York Edition", a 24-volume collection of his works. In 1910 his brother William died; Henry had just joined William from an unsuccessful search for relief in Europe on what then turned out to be his (Henry's) last visit to the United States (from summer 1910 to July 1911), and was near him, according to a letter he wrote, when he died.

In 1913 he wrote his autobiographies, A Small Boy and Others, and Notes of a Son and Brother. After the outbreak of the First World War in 1914 he did war work. In 1915 he became a British subject and was awarded the Order of Merit the following year. He died on 28 February 1916, in Chelsea, London. As he requested, his ashes were buried in Cambridge Cemetery in Massachusetts.

Biographers

James regularly rejected suggestions that he should marry, and after settling in London proclaimed himself "a bachelor". F. W. Dupee, in several volumes on the James family, originated the theory that he had been in love with his cousin Mary ("Minnie") Temple, but that a neurotic fear of sex kept him from admitting such affections: "James's invalidism ... was itself the symptom of some fear of or scruple against sexual love on his part." Dupee used an episode from James's memoir A Small Boy and Others, recounting a dream of a Napoleonic image in the Louvre, to exemplify James's romanticism about Europe, a Napoleonic fantasy into which he fled.

Dupee had not had access to the James family papers and worked principally from James's published memoir of his older brother, William, and the limited collection of letters edited by Percy Lubbock, heavily weighted toward James's last years. His account therefore moved directly from James's childhood, when he trailed after his older brother, to elderly invalidism. As more material became available to scholars, including the diaries of contemporaries and hundreds of affectionate and sometimes erotic letters written by James to younger men, the picture of neurotic celibacy gave way to a portrait of a closeted homosexual.

Between 1953 and 1972, Leon Edel authored a major five-volume biography of James, which accessed unpublished letters and documents after Edel gained the permission of James's family. Edel's portrayal of James included the suggestion he was celibate. It was a view first propounded by critic Saul Rosenzweig in 1943. In 1996 Sheldon M. Novick published Henry James: The Young Master, followed by Henry James: The Mature Master (2007). The first book "caused something of an uproar in Jamesian circles" as it challenged the previous received notion of celibacy, a once-familiar paradigm in biographies of homosexuals when direct evidence was non-existent. Novick also criticised Edel for following the discounted Freudian interpretation of homosexuality "as a kind of failure." The difference of opinion erupted in a series of exchanges between Edel and Novick which were published by the online magazine Slate, with the latter arguing that even the suggestion of celibacy went against James's own injunction "live!"—not "fantasize!"

A letter James wrote in old age to Hugh Walpole has been cited as an explicit statement of this. Walpole confessed to him of indulging in "high jinks", and James wrote a reply endorsing it: "We must know, as much as possible, in our beautiful art, yours & mine, what we are talking about — & the only way to know it is to have lived & loved & cursed & floundered & enjoyed & suffered — I don't think I regret a single 'excess' of my responsive youth".

The interpretation of James as living a less austere emotional life has been subsequently explored by other scholars. The often intense politics of Jamesian scholarship has also been the subject of studies. Author Colm Tóibín has said that Eve Kosofsky Sedgwick's Epistemology of the Closet made a landmark difference to Jamesian scholarship by arguing that he be read as a homosexual writer whose desire to keep his sexuality a secret shaped his layered style and dramatic artistry. According to Tóibín such a reading "removed James from the realm of dead white males who wrote about posh people. He became our contemporary."

James's letters to expatriate American sculptor Hendrik Christian Andersen have attracted particular attention. James met the 27-year-old Andersen in Rome in 1899, when James was 56, and wrote letters to Andersen that are intensely emotional: "I hold you, dearest boy, in my innermost love, & count on your feeling me—in every throb of your soul". In a letter of 6 May 1904, to his brother William, James referred to himself as "always your hopelessly celibate even though sexagenarian Henry". How accurate that description might have been is the subject of contention among James's biographers,   but the letters to Andersen were occasionally quasi-erotic: "I put, my dear boy, my arm around you, & feel the pulsation, thereby, as it were, of our excellent future & your admirable endowment." To his homosexual friend Howard Sturgis, James could write: "I repeat, almost to indiscretion, that I could live with you. Meanwhile I can only try to live without you."

His numerous letters to the many young gay men among his close male friends are more forthcoming. In a letter to Howard Sturgis, following a long visit, James refers jocularly to their "happy little congress of two" and in letters to Hugh Walpole he pursues convoluted jokes and puns about their relationship, referring to himself as an elephant who "paws you oh so benevolently" and winds about Walpole his "well meaning old trunk". His letters to Walter Berry printed by the Black Sun Press have long been celebrated for their lightly veiled eroticism.

He corresponded in almost equally extravagant language with his many female friends, writing, for example, to fellow novelist Lucy Clifford: "Dearest Lucy! What shall I say? when I love you so very, very much, and see you nine times for once that I see Others! Therefore I think that—if you want it made clear to the meanest intelligence—I love you more than I love Others." To his New York friend Mary Cadwalader Jones: "Dearest Mary Cadwalader. I yearn over you, but I yearn in vain; & your long silence really breaks my heart, mystifies, depresses, almost alarms me, to the point even of making me wonder if poor unconscious & doting old Célimare [Jones's pet name for James] has 'done' anything, in some dark somnambulism of the spirit, which has ... given you a bad moment, or a wrong impression, or a 'colourable pretext' ... However these things may be, he loves you as tenderly as ever;

nothing, to the end of time, will ever detach him from you, & he remembers those Eleventh St. matutinal intimes hours, those telephonic matinées, as the most romantic of his life ..." His long friendship with American novelist Constance Fenimore Woolson, in whose house he lived for a number of weeks in Italy in 1887, and his shock and grief over her suicide in 1894, are discussed in detail in Edel's biography and play a central role in a study by Lyndall Gordon. (Edel conjectured that Woolson was in love with James and killed herself in part because of his coldness, but Woolson's biographers have objected to Edel's account.)

Works

Style and themes

James is one of the major figures of trans-Atlantic literature. His works frequently juxtapose characters from the Old World (Europe), embodying a feudal civilisation that is beautiful, often corrupt, and alluring, and from the New World (United States), where people are often brash, open, and assertive and embody the virtues—freedom and a more highly evolved moral character—of the new American society. James explores this clash of personalities and cultures, in stories of personal relationships in which power is exercised well or badly. His protagonists were often young American women facing oppression or abuse, and as his secretary Theodora Bosanquet remarked in her monograph Henry James at Work:

> When he walked out of the refuge of his study and into the world and looked around him, he saw a place of torment, where creatures of prey perpetually thrust their claws into the quivering flesh of doomed, defenseless children of light ... His novels are a repeated exposure of this wickedness, a reiterated and passionate plea for the fullest freedom of development, unimperiled by reckless and barbarous stupidity.

Critics have jokingly described three phases in the development of James's prose: "James I, James II, and The Old Pretender." He wrote short stories and plays. Finally, in his third and last period he returned to the long, serialised novel. Beginning in the second period, but most noticeably in the third, he increasingly abandoned direct statement in favour of frequent double negatives, and complex descriptive imagery. Single paragraphs began to run for page after page, in which an initial noun would be succeeded by pronouns surrounded by clouds of adjectives and prepositional clauses, far from their original referents, and verbs would be deferred and then preceded by a series of adverbs. The overall effect could be a vivid evocation of a scene as perceived by a sensitive observer. It has been debated whether this change of style was engendered by James's shifting from writing to dictating to a typist, a change made during the composition of What Maisie Knew.

In its intense focus on the consciousness of his major characters, James's later work foreshadows extensive developments in 20th century fiction. Indeed, he might have influenced stream-of-consciousness writers such as Virginia Woolf, who not only read some of his novels but also wrote essays about them. Both contemporary and modern readers have found the late style difficult and unnecessary; his friend Edith Wharton, who admired him greatly, said that there were passages in his work that were all but incomprehensible. James was harshly portrayed by H. G. Wells as a hippopotamus laboriously attempting to pick up a pea that had got into a corner of its cage. The "late James" style was ably parodied by Max Beerbohm in "The Mote in the Middle Distance".

More important for his work overall may have been his position as an expatriate, and in other ways an outsider, living in Europe. While he came from middle-class and provincial beginnings (seen from the perspective of European polite society) he worked very hard to gain access to all levels of society, and the settings of his fiction range from working class to aristocratic, and often describe the efforts of middle-class Americans to make their way in European capitals. He confessed he got some of his best story ideas from gossip at the dinner table or at country house weekends. He worked for a living, however, and lacked the experiences of select schools, university, and army service, the common bonds of masculine society. He was furthermore a man whose tastes and interests were, according to the prevailing standards of Victorian era Anglo-American culture, rather feminine, and who was shadowed by the cloud of prejudice that then and later accompanied suspicions of his homosexuality. Edmund Wilson famously compared James's objectivity to Shakespeare's:

One would be in a position to appreciate James better if one compared him with the dramatists of the seventeenth century—Racine and Molière, whom he resembles in form as well as in point of view, and even Shakespeare, when allowances are made for the most extreme differences in subject and form. These poets are not, like Dickens and Hardy, writers of melodrama—either humorous or pessimistic, nor secretaries of society like Balzac, nor prophets like Tolstoy: they are occupied simply with the presentation of conflicts of moral character, which they do not concern themselves about softening or averting. They do not indict society for these situations: they regard them as universal and inevitable. They do not even blame God for allowing them: they accept them as the conditions of life.

It is also possible to see many of James's stories as psychological thought-experiments. In his preface to the New York edition of The American he describes the development of the story in his mind as exactly such: the "situation" of an American, "some robust but insidiously beguiled and betrayed, some cruelly wronged, compatriot..." with the focus of the story being on the response of this wronged man. The Portrait of a Lady may be an experiment to see what happens when an idealistic young woman suddenly becomes very rich. In many of his tales, characters seem to exemplify alternative futures and possibilities, as most markedly in "The Jolly Corner", in which the protagonist and a ghost-doppelganger live alternative American and European lives; and in others, like The Ambassadors, an older James seems fondly to regard his own younger self facing a crucial moment.

Major novels

The first period of James's fiction, usually considered to have culminated in The Portrait of a Lady, concentrated on the contrast between Europe and America. The style of these novels is generally straightforward and, though personally characteristic, well within the norms of 19th-century fiction. Roderick Hudson (1875) is a Künstlerroman that traces the development of the title character, an extremely talented sculptor. Although the book shows some signs of immaturity—this was James's first serious attempt at a full-length novel—it has attracted favourable comment due to the vivid realisation of the three major characters: Roderick Hudson, superbly gifted but unstable and unreliable; Rowland Mallet, Roderick's limited but much more mature friend and patron; and Christina Light, one of James's most enchanting and maddening femmes fatales. The pair of Hudson and Mallet has been seen as representing the two sides of James's own nature: the wildly imaginative artist and the brooding conscientious mentor.

In The Portrait of a Lady (1881) James concluded the first phase of his career with a novel that remains his most popular piece of long fiction. The story is of a spirited young American woman, Isabel Archer, who "affronts her destiny" and finds it overwhelming. She inherits a large amount of money and subsequently becomes the victim of Machiavellian scheming by two American expatriates. The narrative is set mainly in Europe, especially in England and Italy. Generally regarded as the masterpiece of his early phase, The Portrait of a Lady is described as a psychological novel, exploring the minds of his characters, and almost a work of social science, exploring the differences between Europeans and Americans, the old and the new worlds.

The second period of James's career, which extends from the publication of The Portrait of a Lady through the end of the nineteenth century, features less popular novels including The Princess Casamassima, published serially in The Atlantic Monthly in 1885–1886, and The Bostonians, published serially in The Century Magazine during the same period. This period also featured James's celebrated Gothic novella, The Turn of the Screw.

The third period of James's career reached its most significant achievement in three novels published just around the start of the 20th century: The Wings of the Dove (1902), The Ambassadors (1903), and The Golden Bowl (1904). Critic F. O. Matthiessen called this "trilogy" James's major phase, and these novels have certainly received intense critical study. It was the second-written of the books, The Wings of the Dove (1902) that was the first published because it attracted no serialization. This novel tells the story of Milly Theale, an American heiress stricken with a serious disease, and her impact on the people around her. Some of these people befriend Milly with honourable motives, while others are more self-interested. James stated in his autobiographical books that Milly was based on Minny Temple, his beloved cousin who died at an early age of tuberculosis. He said that he attempted in the novel to wrap her memory in the "beauty and dignity of art".

Shorter narratives

James was particularly interested in what he called the "beautiful and blest nouvelle", or the longer form of short narrative. Still, he produced a number of very short stories in which he achieved notable compression of sometimes complex subjects. The following narratives are representative of James's achievement in the shorter forms of fiction.

- "A Tragedy of Error" (1864), short story
- "The Story of a Year" (1865), short story
- A Passionate Pilgrim (1871), novella
- Madame de Mauves (1874), novella
- Daisy Miller (1878), novella
- The Aspern Papers (1888), novella
- The Lesson of the Master (1888), novella
- The Pupil (1891), short story
- "The Figure in the Carpet" (1896), short story
- The Beast in the Jungle (1903), novella
- An International Episode (1878)
- Picture and Text
- Four Meetings (1885)
- A London Life, and Other Tales (1889)
- The Spoils of Poynton (1896)

- Embarrassments (1896)
- The Two Magics: The Turn of the Screw, Covering End (1898)
- A Little Tour of France (1900)
- The Sacred Fount (1901)
- Views and Reviews (1908)
- The Wings of the Dove, Volume I (1902)
- The Wings of the Dove, Volume II (1909)
- The Finer Grain (1910)
- The Outcry (1911)
- Lady Barbarina: The Siege of London, An International Episode and Other Tales (1922)
- The Birthplace (1922)

Plays

At several points in his career James wrote plays, beginning with one-act plays written for periodicals in 1869 and 1871 and a dramatisation of his popular novella Daisy Miller in 1882. From 1890 to 1892, having received a bequest that freed him from magazine publication, he made a strenuous effort to succeed on the London stage, writing a half-dozen plays of which only one, a dramatisation of his novel The American, was produced. This play was performed for several years by a touring repertory company and had a respectable run in London, but did not earn very much money for James. His other plays written at this time were not produced.

In 1893, however, he responded to a request from actor-manager George Alexander for a serious play for the opening of his renovated St. James's Theatre, and wrote a long drama, Guy Domville, which Alexander produced. There was a noisy uproar on the opening night, 5 January 1895, with hissing from the gallery when James took his bow after the final curtain, and the author was upset. The play received moderately good reviews and had a modest run of four weeks before being taken off to make way for Oscar Wilde's The Importance of Being Earnest, which Alexander thought would have better prospects for the coming season.

After the stresses and disappointment of these efforts James insisted that he would write no more for the theatre, but within weeks had agreed to write a curtain-raiser for Ellen Terry. This became the one-act "Summersoft", which he later rewrote into a short story, "Covering End", and then expanded into a full-length play, The High Bid, which had a brief run in London in 1907, when James made another concerted effort to write for the stage. He wrote three new plays, two of which were in production when the death of Edward VII on 6 May 1910 plunged London into mourning and theatres closed. Discouraged by failing health and the stresses of theatrical work, James did not renew his efforts in the theatre, but recycled his plays as successful novels. The Outcry was a best-seller in the United States when it was published in 1911. During the years 1890–1893 when he was most engaged with the theatre, James wrote a good deal of theatrical criticism and assisted Elizabeth Robins and others in translating and producing Henrik Ibsen for the first time in London.

Leon Edel argued in his psychoanalytic biography that James was traumatised by the opening night uproar that greeted Guy Domville, and that it plunged him into a prolonged depression. The successful later novels, in Edel's view, were the result of a kind of self-analysis, expressed in fiction, which partly freed him from his fears. Other biographers and scholars have not accepted this account, however; the more common view being that of F.O. Matthiessen, who wrote: "Instead of being crushed by the collapse of his hopes [for the theatre]... he felt a resurgence of new energy."

Non-fiction

Beyond his fiction, James was one of the more important literary critics in the history of the novel. In his classic essay The Art of Fiction (1884), he argued against rigid prescriptions on the novelist's choice of subject and method of treatment. He maintained that the widest possible freedom in content and approach would help ensure narrative fiction's continued vitality.

James wrote many valuable critical articles on other novelists; typical is his book-length study of Nathaniel Hawthorne, which has been the subject of critical debate. Richard Brodhead has suggested that the study was emblematic of James's struggle with Hawthorne's influence, and constituted an effort to place the elder writer "at a disadvantage." Gordon Fraser, meanwhile, has suggested that the study was part of a more commercial effort by James to introduce himself to British readers as Hawthorne's natural successor.

When James assembled the New York Edition of his fiction in his final years, he wrote a series of prefaces that subjected his own work to searching, occasionally harsh criticism.

At 22 James wrote The Noble School of Fiction for The Nation's first issue in 1865. He would write, in all, over 200 essays and book, art, and theatre reviews for the magazine.

For most of his life James harboured ambitions for success as a playwright. He converted his novel The American into a play that enjoyed modest returns in the early 1890s. In all he wrote about a dozen plays, most of which went unproduced. His costume drama Guy Domville failed disastrously on its opening night in 1895. James then largely abandoned his efforts to conquer the stage and returned to his fiction. In his Notebooks he maintained that his theatrical experiment benefited his novels and tales by helping him dramatise his characters' thoughts and emotions. James produced a small but valuable amount of theatrical criticism, including perceptive appreciations of Henrik Ibsen.

With his wide-ranging artistic interests, James occasionally wrote on the visual arts. Perhaps his most valuable contribution was his favourable assessment of fellow expatriate John Singer Sargent, a painter whose critical status has improved markedly in recent decades. James also wrote sometimes charming, sometimes brooding articles about various places he visited and lived in. His most famous books of travel writing include Italian Hours (an example of the charming approach) and The American Scene (most definitely on the brooding side).

James was one of the great letter-writers of any era. More than ten thousand of his personal letters are extant, and over three thousand have been published in a large number of collections. A complete edition of James's letters began publication in 2006, edited by Pierre Walker and Greg Zacharias. As of 2014, eight volumes have been published, covering the period from 1855 to 1880. James's correspondents included celebrated contemporaries like Robert Louis Stevenson, Edith Wharton and Joseph Conrad, along with many others in his wide circle of friends and acquaintances. The letters range from the "mere twaddle of graciousness" to serious discussions of artistic, social and personal issues.

Very late in life James began a series of autobiographical works: A Small Boy and Others, Notes of a Son and Brother, and the unfinished The Middle Years. These books portray the development of a classic observer who was passionately interested in artistic creation but was somewhat reticent about participating fully in the life around him.

Reception

Criticism, biographies and fictional treatments

James's work has remained steadily popular with the limited audience of educated readers to whom he spoke during his lifetime, and has remained firmly in the canon, but, after his death, some American critics, such as Van Wyck Brooks, expressed hostility towards James for his long expatriation and eventual naturalisation as a British subject. Other critics such as E. M. Forster complained about what they saw as James's squeamishness in the treatment of sex and other possibly controversial material, or dismissed his late style as difficult and obscure, relying heavily on extremely long sentences and excessively latinate language. Similarly Oscar Wilde criticised him for writing "fiction as if it were a painful duty". Vernon Parrington, composing a canon of American literature, condemned James for having cut himself off from America. Jorge Luis Borges wrote about him, "Despite the scruples and delicate complexities of James, his work suffers from a major defect: the absence of life." And Virginia Woolf, writing to Lytton Strachey, asked, "Please tell me what you find in Henry James. ... we have his works here, and

I read, and I can't find anything but faintly tinged rose water, urbane and sleek, but vulgar and pale as Walter Lamb. Is there really any sense in it?" The novelist W. Somerset Maugham wrote, "He did not know the English as an Englishman instinctively knows them and so his English characters never to my mind quite ring true," and argued "The great novelists, even in seclusion, have lived life passionately. Henry James was content to observe it from a window." Maugham nevertheless wrote, "The fact remains that those last novels of his, notwithstanding their unreality, make all other novels, except the very best, unreadable." Colm Tóibín observed that James "never really wrote about the English very well. His English characters don't work for me."

Despite these criticisms, James is now valued for his psychological and moral realism, his masterful creation of character, his low-key but playful humour, and his assured command of the language. In his 1983 book, The Novels of Henry James, Edward Wagenknecht offers an assessment that echoes Theodora Bosanquet's:

"To be completely great," Henry James wrote in an early review, "a work of art must lift up the heart," and his own novels do this to an outstanding degree ... More than sixty years after his death, the great novelist who sometimes professed to have no opinions stands foursquare in the great Christian humanistic and democratic tradition. The men and women who, at the height of World War II, raided the secondhand shops for his out-of-print books knew what they were about. For no writer ever raised a braver banner to which all who love freedom might adhere.

William Dean Howells saw James as a representative of a new realist school of literary art which broke with the English romantic tradition epitomised by the works of Charles Dickens and William Makepeace Thackeray. Howells wrote that realism found "its chief exemplar in Mr. James... A novelist he is not, after the old fashion, or after any fashion but his own." F.R. Leavis championed Henry James as a novelist of "established pre-eminence" in The Great Tradition (1948), asserting that The Portrait of a Lady and The Bostonians were "the two most brilliant novels in the language." James is now prized as a master of point of view who moved literary fiction forward by insisting in showing, not telling, his stories to the reader. (Source: Wikipedia)

NOTABLE WORKS

NOVELS

Watch and Ward (1871)

Roderick Hudson (1875)

The American (1877)

The Europeans (1878)

Confidence (1879)

Washington Square (1880)

The Portrait of a Lady (1881)

The Bostonians (1886)

The Princess Casamassima (1886)

The Reverberator (1888)

The Tragic Muse (1890)

The Other House (1896)

The Spoils of Poynton (1897)

What Maisie Knew (1897)

The Awkward Age (1899)

The Sacred Fount (1901)

The Wings of the Dove (1902)

The Ambassadors (1903)

The Golden Bowl (1904)

The Whole Family (collaborative novel with eleven other authors, 1908)

The Outcry (1911)

The Ivory Tower (unfinished, published posthumously 1917)

The Sense of the Past (unfinished, published posthumously 1917)

SHORT STORIES AND NOVELLAS

A Tragedy of Error (1864)

The Story of a Year (1865)

A Landscape Painter (1866)

A Day of Days (1866)

My Friend Bingham (1867)

Poor Richard (1867)

The Story of a Masterpiece (1868)

A Most Extraordinary Case (1868)

A Problem (1868)

De Grey: A Romance (1868)

Osborne's Revenge (1868)

The Romance of Certain Old Clothes (1868)

A Light Man (1869)

Gabrielle de Bergerac (1869)

Travelling Companions (1870)

A Passionate Pilgrim (1871)

At Isella (1871)

Master Eustace (1871)

Guest's Confession (1872)

The Madonna of the Future (1873)

The Sweetheart of M. Briseux (1873)

The Last of the Valerii (1874)

Madame de Mauves (1874)

Adina (1874)

Professor Fargo (1874)

Eugene Pickering (1874)

Benvolio (1875)

Crawford's Consistency (1876)

The Ghostly Rental (1876)

Four Meetings (1877)

Rose-Agathe (1878, as Théodolinde)

Daisy Miller (1878)

Longstaff's Marriage (1878)

An International Episode (1878)

The Pension Beaurepas (1879)

A Diary of a Man of Fifty (1879)

A Bundle of Letters (1879)

The Point of View (1882)

The Siege of London (1883)

Impressions of a Cousin (1883)

Lady Barberina (1884)

Pandora (1884)

The Author of Beltraffio (1884)

Georgina's Reasons (1884)

A New England Winter (1884)

The Path of Duty (1884)

Mrs. Temperly (1887)

Louisa Pallant (1888)

The Aspern Papers (1888)

The Liar (1888)

The Modern Warning (1888, originally published as The Two Countries)

A London Life (1888)

The Patagonia (1888)

The Lesson of the Master (1888)

The Solution (1888)

The Pupil (1891)

Brooksmith (1891)

The Marriages (1891)

The Chaperon (1891)

Sir Edmund Orme (1891)

Nona Vincent (1892)

The Real Thing (1892)

The Private Life (1892)

Lord Beaupré (1892)

The Visits (1892)

Sir Dominick Ferrand (1892)

Greville Fane (1892)

Collaboration (1892)

Owen Wingrave (1892)

The Wheel of Time (1892)

The Middle Years (1893)

The Death of the Lion (1894)

The Coxon Fund (1894)

The Next Time (1895)

Glasses (1896)

The Altar of the Dead (1895)

The Figure in the Carpet (1896)

The Way It Came (1896, also published as The Friends of the Friends)

The Turn of the Screw (1898)

Covering End (1898)

In the Cage (1898)

John Delavoy (1898)

The Given Case (1898)

Europe (1899)

The Great Condition (1899)

The Real Right Thing (1899)

Paste (1899)

The Great Good Place (1900)

Maud-Evelyn (1900)

Miss Gunton of Poughkeepsie (1900)

The Tree of Knowledge (1900)

The Abasement of the Northmores (1900)

The Third Person (1900)

The Special Type (1900)

The Tone of Time (1900)

Broken Wings (1900)

The Two Faces (1900)

Mrs. Medwin (1901)

The Beldonald Holbein (1901)

The Story in It (1902)

Flickerbridge (1902)

The Birthplace (1903)

The Beast in the Jungle (1903)

The Papers (1903)

Fordham Castle (1904)

Julia Bride (1908)

The Jolly Corner (1908)

The Velvet Glove (1909)

Mora Montravers (1909)

Crapy Cornelia (1909)

The Bench of Desolation (1909)

A Round of Visits (1910)

OTHER

Transatlantic Sketches (1875)

French Poets and Novelists (1878)

Hawthorne (1879)

Portraits of Places (1883)

A Little Tour in France (1884)

Partial Portraits (1888)

Essays in London and Elsewhere (1893)

Picture and Text (1893)

Terminations (1893)

Theatricals (1894)

Theatricals: Second Series (1895)

Guy Domville (1895)

The Soft Side (1900)

William Wetmore Story and His Friends (1903)

The Better Sort (1903)

English Hours (1905)

The Question of our Speech; The Lesson of Balzac. Two Lectures (1905)

The American Scene (1907)

Views and Reviews (1908)

Italian Hours (1909)

A Small Boy and Others (1913)

Notes on Novelists (1914)

Notes of a Son and Brother (1914)

Within the Rim (1918)

Travelling Companions (1919)

Notebooks (various, published posthumously)

The Middle Years (unfinished, published posthumously 1917)

A Most Unholy Trade (1925, published posthumously)

The Art of the Novel : Critical Prefaces (1934)